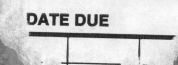

Borrowed Children

A Richard Jackson Book

Borrowed Children

GEORGE ELLA LYON

ORCHARD BOOKS   NEW YORK   LONDON

A division of Franklin Watts, Inc.

Orchard Books
387 Park Avenue South
New York, New York 10016

Orchard Books Great Britain
10 Golden Square
London W1R 3AF England

Orchard Books Australia
14 Mars Road
Lane Cove, New South Wales 2066

Orchard Books Canada
20 Torbay Road
Markham, Ontario 23P 1G6

Orchard Books is a division of Franklin Watts, Inc.

Manufactured in the United States of America
Book design by Mina Greenstein
The text of this book is set in 11 pt. Fournier.
1 2 3 4 5 6 7 8 9 10

Library of Congress Cataloging-in-Publication Data
Lyon, George Ella, 1949–
Borrowed children by George Ella Lyon.
Summary: Having been forced to act as mother and housekeeper
during Mama's illness, twelve-year-old Amanda has a holiday in
Memphis, far removed from the Depression drudgery of her Kentucky
mountain family, and finds her world expanding even as she grows
to understand and appreciate her own background.
ISBN 0-531-05751-8. ISBN 0-531-08351-9 (lib. bdg.)
[1. Depressions—1929—Fiction. 2. Mountain life—Fiction. 3.
Family life—Fiction. 4. Kentucky—Fiction. 5. Memphis
(Tenn.)—Fiction.] I. Title.
PZ7.L9954IBo 1988 87-22700 CIP AC [Fic]—dc19

FOR MY MOTHER

*"Don't you think you were a fine woman
for me to study, to learn by heart?"*
—*"Riding Hood"*
BETSY SHOLL

1

 It's Friday. Fridays are the best days because
we know Daddy is coming home. He works
all week cutting timber on Big Lick Mountain—too far to come back to Goose Rock every night.
I wish he could. The house lights up when Daddy's
here.

Even now, just knowing he's on his way, chores
seem easier and we don't quarrel. I've been taking care
of my little sisters, Anna and Helen, but they've been
happy—Helen stringing spools on yarn, Anna looking
at the new Sears-Roebuck catalogue. "Wish Book,"
Daddy calls it. "Wishes are free," he says. "Look your
fill." And we do. They've got things on those slick
pages that Goose Rock's never seen: clothes washers,
typewriters, electric lights. But Anna looks at dolls.

"I'd give a bushel of money for that bride doll," she
says, pointing to a tall one got up in wads of lace.

"And what would you do with her? She'd be thick
with coal dust in no time." In Goose Rock coal dust
is as common as dirt.

"I'd keep her under my pillow," Anna insists.

"And squash her flat as a board."

"Oh, Mandy . . ."

"Remember what Daddy said about Miss Snavely and the Wish Book. You don't always get what you order."

"What did he say?"

"Said she ordered a suit, and when it came, her heart broke because it didn't have that pretty man in it."

"That's just a story," Anna argues. "Nobody's that dumb."

"No? Then what are they doing here, stuck between two mountains with nothing but a Wish Book to look at?"

"We're not dumb and we're here."

"That's because we follow the timber."

"Maybe it's the trees that are dumb," Helen suggests.

"That's it exactly," I tell her. "Dumb maple! Dumb walnut! Knot-head pine."

We're all laughing when Ben bursts in.

"Mandy, I've got to talk to you," he says, his breath coming in heaves. "Right now. Private." He motions me out on the porch.

Ben is fourteen, tall and skinny like me, but that's okay for a boy. He's been running, and his hair looks like a blackbird about to take off.

"I'm listening," I say, glancing through the window to make sure the girls don't knock over a lamp or something.

"You know those lunches Mama packs us in school-time—ham biscuit, a jar of milk? Well, that's all right here in Goose Rock, but when you go to Manchester to school . . . why, there's boys eating steak between white bread, Mandy, and not out of paper sacks either. They say you can buy that bread sliced and it tastes just like cake. And there we sit with dry biscuits and hard ham. So me and David—I don't know which of us first—we just thought we'd go to the hotel one day and try out lunch there."

I can't believe it. David's two years older than Ben and so crazy about Polly Anderson I didn't know he'd even noticed the Asher Hotel. I've wanted to eat there ever since I first laid eyes on it—white and tall and fancy, like a hotel in New York. I've read about New York, you know. And that's the kind of place I belong. But I'd be too scared—not of the hotel people but of Mama and Daddy—to ever just walk in.

"Well, what was it like?"

"You never saw a thing like it," Ben says, his blue eyes warming, "unless it was in the dining car bound for Memphis. Tablecloths and silver dish covers, hot meat and potatoes with the butter standing. Why, we ate so much, David said he slept through the next hour of school. Not me. And Mr. Asher told us to come back to the hotel any time we wanted, he was proud to do business with Mr. Perritt's sons."

"Proud to take Daddy's money, you mean." Ben's face whitens. I didn't mean to make him feel worse. "That's pretty bad," I say, "but anybody can slip up once. Daddy'll get over it."

"But it wasn't just once," Ben says, his voice rising.

'We went there the whole last month of school, Mandy, and that's how come Mr. Asher sent Daddy a bill. It's come today. Mama said she couldn't think what we owed the hotel for."

"And she's not opened it?"

"I reckon not. I can still sit down."

"Well, try not to worry," I tell him. "It may blow over."

His eyes follow mine to a thunderhead along the ridge.

Without a word, he bolts off the porch, then lopes across the yard and through the narrow meadow to the shed. I expect that's where he ran in from. Had to go talk to Welkie about the bill before he talked to me. Welkie's a horse. Ben gets more comfort out of any kind of creature than most people do from best friends.

He's going to need comfort too. Money is already a problem around here. Sawmill business is down because of something called the Depression, and Mama is expecting another baby. Don't ask me why. A baby is the last thing we need.

So it's going to hit hard, this bill from the Asher Hotel. Ben and David never should have done it. As long as they did, though, I wish they'd taken me along. I'm the one who would appreciate it. Boys judge a meal by how well it covers the plate.

It's getting dark as a cellar out here and it's only six o'clock. Daddy says these are dog days—hot enough to make anybody pant. But now a wind's come up and the forsythia bush skitters against the porch. Mama calls to ask if I see Daddy, and I go in, watching the curtains blow at the window.

"Not a sign," I tell her.

He should be here by now. The table's laid, the dumplings puffing up in the chicken broth. Mama's lit the lamp above the gold-rimmed tureen on the table.

"It's chipped but it's gold," she says, patting the graceful lid, "and older than any of us. Came over with the Ezelles from France, packed in feathers."

My grandmother Omie was an Ezelle, and Mama always says this whenever we have chicken and dumplings or stew or whatever requires the tureen. I like to think of the Ezelles themselves packed in feathers.

I follow her back to the kitchen. It's strange—I'm taller than she is now. I check the part in her hair. Always straight. Everything about her is neat, plump, and pretty. Where did she get a daughter like a clothesline pole?

Sweat beads on her forehead as she mixes the cornbread batter.

"No point in baking this till your father gets here. Go see if you see him coming."

As I pass through the parlor, Helen reaches for something in the catalogue, Anna jerks it back, and the thin page rips.

"She's tearing up my dolls!" Anna hollers.

"Mine, too!" Helen holds the crumpled paper close.

"Take them outside, Amanda," Mama says. "Leave the catalogue and go watch for Daddy. It'll help him get home. Somebody watching always does."

So we troop out to the porch. Thunder rumbles like

empty coal cars. Just as we reach the rail, the rain comes down in buckets and lightning bleaches the dirt road in front of our house. All of a sudden there's a shriek, Helen grabs me around the waist, and Anna starts pointing and screaming. I look where she's looking and see a horse and rider blurred by the slant of rain.

"It's all right," I begin.

"But *look* at him," Anna splutters. "It can't be Daddy. He doesn't have a . . ."

Then I see what she sees. The figure sits high, his body covered in a cape. And where his head should be, there's nothing. It's like in the Sleepy Hollow story— but this time it's coming at a gallop directly for us.

The screen door bangs and I feel Mama behind us. I reach for her hand, but she's already holding Helen's, so I grab the rail. The figure is getting close now, swaying and gleaming.

Not a one of us moves and even Helen is quiet. The figure slows, dismounts, and leads the horse toward the porch. Mama takes a step forward, drawing herself up. "Come no farther," she commands.

Then the rider throws back its shoulders and laughs. It keeps coming. The cloak slips down, a head emerges, and it's Daddy, his smile wide, his glasses all steamed up.

I almost cry, I'm so glad it's him, but Helen buries her face in my skirt. Mama moves toward him, not yet ready to laugh.

"Jim," she says, "what on earth do you think you're doing, scaring the children to death?"

Now he's up on the porch, water pouring off the cloak, and him still shaking with laughter.

"Just trying to keep dry," he says. "I cut a piece of cloth off a log tarp. Never dreamed it would give these girls a fright. I couldn't see them through the rain."

"Well, they could see you," Mama says, "and you could have been the Devil himself." She's trying to brush water off his face. "I'll call one of the boys to come get Midge."

"That's all right, Rena." Daddy lays a dripping hand on her shoulder. "I'll walk on down to the shed."

Mama doesn't smile till his back is turned, and then it's a slow smile, like the sun coming up.

"You girls get on in the house now," she says. "It's so damp out here you could catch your death."

2

And so she herds us in—through the parlor and the dining room to the back of the kitchen.

Towels hang by the washtub where we bathe. I dry Helen off while Anna gives herself a rubdown. I didn't realize the rain had blown in on us so much. Guess I was too scared.

Mama dabs at her face with her apron, then scrapes cornbread batter into a cast-iron skillet which she eases into the stove.

If this were a regular Friday we could relax now. But there's that bill, hanging over everything. I wonder if Ben's trying to break it to Daddy down at the shed. And I wonder about David. He won't take whatever happens as hard as Ben, or he won't show it. David's calm as snow.

Here they come now, up the back steps.

"Scrape your feet, boys," Daddy orders.

Stamping and tramping like mules, they come in. I pass the towels. When Daddy takes off his glasses to wipe his face, it's so naked and tired, I look away. From behind the towel he begins:

"The boys tell me the hotel sent us a bill, Rena. You haven't been putting up secret Memphis kin?"

"Not chick nor child," she answers, bent over, checking the fire in the stove.

"Probably Mr. Asher's mistake." He sets his glasses on his nose, then anchors them behind his ears. "But I'd best have a look."

He walks out of the kitchen and his good mood all at once. Ben blanches; David studies his hands.

The hinge creaks as Daddy opens Mama's desk in the parlor. A pause while he find the bill and the letter knife. Then:

"God almighty, what has been going on?"

Mama goes through that door, too.

"What is it, Mandy?" Anna always thinks I know. "What's wrong?"

"You tell her, David," I say.

But Daddy's back, taller and louder than he left.

"I want an explanation, boys, and it had better be good."

"Mandy," Mama starts.

"I know. Take the girls to their room. But I'd like to—"

"Do as I say."

So we miss the big scene.

"David and Ben did something wrong," I tell Anna, after she and Helen are sitting on the edge of our bed.

We're not allowed to lie on it unless we pull back

the red and white zigzag quilt, Hard Road to Kansas. Daddy said his mama called it Drunkard's Path.

"Did *what* wrong?" Anna demands, pushing her brown hair out of her eyes. It's straight as straw.

Daddy's voice rolls down the hall:

"You think I cut down money trees on Big Lick?"

I try to cover it over.

"Well, you know David and Ben go to the high school in Manchester now?"

Anna nods. Helen slides to the floor, chewing on the blond sprig of her braid.

"And they take their lunch, just like we do?"

She nods again.

"Trouble is, toward the end of school, they quit eating it. Started going to the Asher Hotel for lunch instead. The bill's for that."

"Oh. That's trouble, huh?"

It's my turn to nod.

"And they're going to get a whipping?"

"At least."

"They're awfully big," Anna ventures.

"So was their mistake."

The screen door bangs. More heavy feet on the back steps.

"I guess the discussion's over," I tell them. "Mama will call us in a minute."

"Mandy?" Helen's voice surprises me from the floor. "Has Daddy ever whipped you?"

"No. But Mama's switches sure have made me dance."

"Will Daddy whip them with his belt?"

"I don't know, Helen. What's wrong?" Her wide mouth is twitching to cry.

"What will they do? They can't eat with us or go in the wagon. . . ." Big tears roll down her cheeks.

"Helen, what are you talking about?" It's Anna asking this time.

"If they can't sit down," Helen explains. "David said if Daddy used his belt, they'd never sit down again."

"Oh, honey," I kneel beside her. Anna giggles. "They don't mean *really*. They just mean they'll be sore."

This is the child who ran out to look when Mama said her birthday was just around the corner.

"You girls wash up," Mama calls. "Mandy, come pour the milk."

Dinner is slow and silent. Helen drops her cornbread. I pick it up quick and Mama pretends not to see. Before anyone asks for seconds, David mumbles:

"May we be excused?"

"There's applesauce for dessert," Mama says.

"Thanks, but I've had enough."

Ben agrees.

"Well, then, go along."

And they do, walking very carefully, like they had somebody else's legs.

Once they're out of the room, Daddy declares, "Not a nickel of that bill do I mean to pay. Tomorrow I'll go into town and speak to Lige Asher. He's bound to have some work those boys can do. They'll see more of that hotel than they reckoned on."

He folds his napkin and puts it beside his plate.

"Rena, if you'll excuse me now, I've got a little figuring to do."

"I'll bring your coffee."

Nodding thanks, he goes back to the desk.

Daddy likes to carve, and usually on Friday nights he takes up whatever piece he's working on and sits in the kitchen whittling, while Mama and I do the dishes. But not tonight. The parlor could be as far away as the mill.

"Finish up, girls," Mama tells us. But the dumplings are heavy and cold.

"I'm too full," I say.

"You'll see it again tomorrow." We nod. "Then let's get the kitchen done," she says. "Bad business cooking for them that won't eat."

3

 David and Ben started working at the Asher on Sunday. They won't tell what they did, but Ben says it was "too close to housework" for him.

That makes me mad. It's easy for them to scorn clothes-washing and floor-scrubbing and chicken-plucking. It's all done for them—I even make up their bed! And Mama's silly about them; she always has been: David because he's her firstborn and Ben because he's so much like Daddy as a boy. At least that's what *she* thinks:

"I just look at him and catch up on all of Jim Perritt I missed."

And Ben doesn't look any more like Daddy than a frog.

"It's his walk," she says. "It's how he looks out of his eyes."

So I'm glad they're getting a little taste of dust rags and paste wax. I hope Mr. Asher has them do everything that's to be done. Puts them in little aprons.

Makes them wear maid hats. I'd walk the four miles to town just to see it!

They've got to work all this week, which is the last one before school starts. Then they'll go in on Saturdays for a while. I wonder if all those fancy lunches were worth it.

Mama and I are busy getting clothes ready for school. Monday we altered and mended, yesterday we washed, and today we're ironing. We're set up in the kitchen with basket, clothes, the board, and three irons—one to heat up while the other cools from use, and a small one for finishing.

"No child of mine is going to drag around like a ragamuffin," she says, as though that's a fate you have to fight all the time. "You're lucky, Mandy. You're the one with new clothes."

But *new* isn't exactly the word. Mama's sister, Aunt Laura, sent a box of her discarded clothes from Memphis. That's where Omie lives too. It's not that the clothes aren't nice—they're too nice is the problem: a black file suit, nipped at the waist; a water-blue taffeta skirt; a slick red dress with hardly a front.

"How could she wear that?" I ask Mama.

"Well, Laura's endowed," she says.

"Endowed? You mean with money?"

Mama smiles.

"No, I mean her bust is full enough that she fills this out. Of course, it's still a bit scandalous, but Laura is Laura."

Mama's still smiling, then shrugs the smile away.

"At any rate, with a little white yoke I can fill it in for you. And the suit just needs to be hemmed."

"Oh, Mama, I can't go to school in clothes like that!"

"And why not? They're perfectly decent clothes. Or will be."

"But nobody wears clothes like that! And I'm not— I don't even fill out a slip."

Mama pats her stomach, where the dress is stretched like a skin.

"Well, I certainly do."

I don't know what to say to that.

"And you'll look better in Laura's clothes than you will in your birthday suit. You've grown too much over the summer to wear most of last year's clothes. Besides, Mandy, by the end of this year you don't know how you'll look. You're getting to an age—" Her voice trails off. She gestures for me to bring her the hot iron from the stove.

"What do you mean?" I ask, setting the hot weight down, taking back the cool one.

For a minute Mama just looks at me.

"You'll be starting to mature is all," she says. Then she sprinkles water from a jar onto the iron to test its heat.

I want to ask more, but her face says the talk is finished. It's the same with the clothes. No point in arguing. So I go on dipping shirts in starch and rolling them into balls. And I keep an eye on Anna and Helen through the screen door. They're in the back yard shelling beans.

School will be all right somehow, though. It always is. Just thinking about it makes my throat tighten. "Pencil fever," Daddy calls it when I can't wait to go back to school. "Darnedest thing I ever saw."

Daddy finished the eighth grade and Mama went on into high school, so they know what it's like. Except they didn't have Mr. Aden for a teacher. If they had, they might have caught pencil fever too.

Mr. Aden's from Boston. He came to Goose Rock on a mission, he says, but he and the Almighty got separated on the way down, so he doesn't work for a church.

"I work for *you*," he tells us, "for the tilling of your minds and the fruit of your ever-growing souls."

I told Mama and Daddy that.

"Bet he gets a check, too," Daddy said.

Sure he does, but that's not the main thing. Mr. Aden has a greater goal in life than "worshiping the brazen dollar." That's why he came to the mountains.

"People are different here," he says.

Daddy says we can't worship what we haven't got.

I expect Mr. Aden just got tired of Boston, the way a full person pushes back his plate. But that wouldn't happen to me. I'm hungry enough to feast on a city forever: theaters and cobbled streets, museums and libraries and running water! We have to pump our water in Goose Rock, of course, and order books from Sears-Roebuck. That means we don't get many. A library means *free* books, all you want, over and over.

"You'll have a library here," Mr. Aden promised us. "The spirit requires books and there will be money for them once people's bodily needs are met. We must be patient. In the meantime, I'll make a school library of my collection."

And that's what he did. The first week I brought home *Jane Eyre*. . . .

"Amanda!"

"Oh—what, Mama?"

"I've been talking to you for five minutes and I don't believe you've heard a word."

"I'm sorry. I guess I was daydreaming."

"Well, those shirts are going to turn to bricks if you don't hand them over here. And these I've finished need to be hung up in the boys' room."

I've exchanged the wet rolls of cloth for the billowing shirts when I hear a knock at the door. A steady knock, insistent.

"My word, who could that be?" Mama says, putting down the iron, smoothing her dress front with her hands.

"Amanda, you wait here."

From the kitchen I watch her heavy journey around the dining room table and into the parlor. I can't see the front door.

"May I help you?"

"Mrs. Perritt?" a husky young voice asks.

"Yes?"

"I'm Cob Russell, Wilt Russell's son, from Russell's Grocery, you know, in Manchester . . ."

"Yes?" For some reason, she lets him fumble.

"And I need to talk to you about business."

"Come right in then."

"Particular business," the voice adds, as though that makes the situation clear.

"Won't you have a seat?" Mama offers.

"No." His voice jerks. "That is, this won't take but a minute."

"Very well,"

"It's, it's this bill: we've carried you over for three months and, well, you've always been solid customers, but . . ."

"I paid that bill," Mama says, her words separate and firm as stones.

Paper rattles. Cob Russell seems to be hunting.

"Yes," he agrees, "but this check—your bank won't cover it."

"May I see it, please?"

Making sure the girls are still at their task, I tiptoe into the parlor and across to the corner where I can see him hand her the check.

She looks at it, nods in recognition, and then, cool as you please, tears it up. Confetti floats through his open hand.

"You needn't come out here again," she tells him. "We will pay what we owe."

He just stands there with his jaw dropped.

Mama starts for the door and he stumbles after her. I duck into the kitchen, busying myself with shirts.

A minute later, Mama comes back. "Well, young lady," she says, dusting off her hands, "have you seen enough?"

4

I expect Mama to be mad at me for eavesdropping, but she's more concerned with what's happened.

"Imagine Mr. Russell sending that boy out here, all puffed up like a fritter! He knows we always pay."

"But what was wrong with the check?"

"I expect I wrote it too soon. You see, your father has a separate account for the mill and has to transfer funds from that account to—well, it's too complicated for you to worry with. The basic thing is the money was there, it was just in the wrong place."

"So Mr. Russell will be paid?"

"Of course. The money will be in his hands tomorrow. You just forget it and come help me with this."

She has a pair of work pants half hauled out of the basket and needs me to untangle it from a knot of other clothes. I study her face. She doesn't *look* like she's lying.

"When I finish this," she says, sprinkling the khaki,

"we'll have some lunch. You round up the girls and get them washed."

Out I go, obedient as a dog. There are the cane-bottomed chairs, which I set in the yard because the ground wasps are swarming; there are the bean sack, the hulls, and the bowl of dull white beans. But no Anna and Helen. I take off running to the spring, Anna's favorite place.

From the top of the slope, I can see them on the flat rock, one brown head, one blond, bent over something intently. Farther down I catch the glint of a syrup bucket lid passed from one to the other. A tea party. No doubt Stella and Mabel Baby are the propped-up guests.

"Anna!" I holler. Then, coming closer: "What do you mean taking off like that, without even asking?"

She looks up, her eyes buckeye brown.

"You and Mama weren't in the kitchen," she starts, "and I'd finished the beans, so . . ."

"Well, you should have come to find me. I have to know where you are, okay? Otherwise, Mama will skin us all."

She nods.

"Come on now. Sun says it's time for lunch."

I gather up the dolls, toss the leaf-cakes off the bright lid.

"Mandy?" Helen's voice is thin as a thread. "Can I take these to Mama?"

She holds up a clutch of wilted chickory.

"Sure. She'll love them."

"And when we have our nap, will you tell us a story?"

"I always tell you a story."

"I know, but would you tell the one about finding the baby?"

I agree to that, too. But I wonder, as we scramble up to the house, what to make of that story. Do I still believe it?

"Once upon a time," I begin an hour later, sweating in our darkened room, "there was a baby. A girl. What little hair she had was dark and her eyes were dark also. She had a pink mouth—not like a rosebud—more like a blackberry stain. For she was born in July. But she was born in a city far away."

"Where?" Anna interrupts.

"I don't know. Maybe Boston. You lie down. Now her parents had a beautiful house, near the theater, with a maid and a silky dog, and a dove-gray motor car. But they couldn't keep their baby. It isn't clear why. Perhaps the father had caught a disease from the city and the mother had to take care of him. And they wanted their little girl to grow up far away from hard streets and smoky skies.

"So they asked a friend of theirs who was making a business trip down south to take the baby and leave her, with a packet of money, in some beautiful spot, near a family with a touch of refinement. And that friend just happened to take the L & N railroad and then, for a lark, the Manchester spur. And from there he took a little buggy—I don't know. Anyway, he came to a field with goldenrod blooming and blackberries on the vine. There was a house nearby, with a woman hanging wash and two little boys in overalls on the porch.

" 'There's a home for this baby,' he thought to himself. 'That family looks to be in need of a little girl.' "

"Was it me?" Helen asks. "Was it me they needed?"

"Shhhhh!" Anna hisses.

"And he found a shady spot, not too close to the blackberries because of bees, and there he put the baby basket down. Right near the path to the cow pasture, so they'd find her by evening for sure. And, with a few extra coos for the baby, off he went.

"Later, one of the little boys saw the basket down the hill. 'Mama's left the wash in a funny place,' he thought. And down he ran to check on it. What should he find but a beautiful brown-haired baby, red-faced from sleeping in the sun? (For the sun had shifted since the man left her there.) And David—the boy was called David—bounded up the hill to his mother, who was sitting in the porch swing, breaking beans.

" 'Mama, Mama! It's a baby! I've found a baby! Come quick!'

"And the mama folded the beans into the newspaper in her lap and rose and came the short way down the hill, without even a hat. And sure enough, she saw just what David had seen. But she picked the baby up.

" 'Oh, you poor hot thing!' she crooned. 'You poor little sugar plum. Who would have left you here?' "

Helen, eyes closed, hugs Mabel Baby tight.

"And she carried the baby to the house, with David behind her dragging the basket as best he could.

"Was there a note in the basket? Yes, there was, to avoid legal troubles. It gave the girl-child to the finder of the basket, provided she or he would give it a good home. It asked for Christian love and forbearance, and for good books and elegant clothes, when possible. And it pointed out that there was a handsome sum of money sewn into a pillow in the basket.

"But the pillow wasn't in the basket. Indeed, it was never found. Had the 'friend' delivered the child and then made off with his 'fee'? Had the packet fallen from the basket as it was carried from car to train through stations, to smaller trains, and finally to the buggy and across the field? Was it lost somewhere in the meadow grass? Would it turn up someday? Nobody knew.

"What the Perritts and their neighbors did know was that there was this sudden baby. She had good digestion and slept well. But since they didn't understand her story, they decided not to tell it. They decided to raise her as their own. . . .

"Anna?" No answer. "Helen?"

Usually at the end of this story, they're full of questions: Who was the baby? Was it our David who found her? Where is she now? And I make up different answers with each telling. But today they're sound asleep, worn out by a sack of beans. And I'm left with my own questions. Did I dream this story? It seems like I've always known it, always known, whatever creek we've lived on, that I didn't belong. I've wanted something Wish Books didn't carry—finer than cornbread, higher than any ridge. How could I be like that, born to Mama and Daddy? How did I get here if the story isn't true?

5

Sometimes I think housework comes down to hot water: laundry, canning, chicken scalding. Today we're making jelly and chow-chow, but first we have to fetch the Mason jars.

Helen's too little and scared to go down to the cellar, but Anna does her part.

"Oooo," she squeals. "It's creepy down here."

"You should be the first one down and have to light the lantern."

"It's like a cave."

"It *is* a cave. A cave with shelves."

More than half the shelves are already clean and loaded: fat red tomatoes, gold corn, olive green beans. There are June apples, too, fried or cooked into sauce, and pears and blackberries. With fall will come spiced apples, apple butter, and a jar of brandied cherries. That's for Christmas. But today it's jelly.

The jars rattle as we carry them up the steps. Old spider webs net our hair.

I feel Anna about to holler.

"Keep your mouth shut," I warn. "It'll get on your tongue, too."

When we get back to the kitchen, Mama takes the hairbrush to us. Then she sets Anna to washing the jars, Helen the lids and rings. I'm the scalder. We're all sweat-shiny by the time Mama ladles purple syrup into the clean jars.

"It'll jell as it cools," she promises. "And tomorrow you can take some to the Skidmores."

I knew that was coming.

"Don't roll your eyes at me, young lady."

I meant to close them before they rolled.

"Maggie Skidmore is a kind Christian soul and it won't hurt you one bit to take her her due. She gave us the grapes, you know."

Oh, but it will hurt me. I *hate* going to the Skidmores'. Their house is worse than the cellar—dark and smelly and piled with unknown stuff. I'd rather do without jelly than owe it to the Skidmores.

Mama looks with satisfaction at the filled jars.

"Like jewels," she says. "Amethysts or garnets."

Then her gaze shifts to me.

"You won't scorn the Skidmores when you taste this on hot bread."

She's right about that. And I know Mrs. Skidmore has more than her share of troubles: a mean husband, triplets, and only one arm. The triplets are regular demons, and she can't catch them enough to teach them different. At least Mama has her babies one at a time.

"It sure looks good," I say.

Really the wobbly jelly turns my stomach. I'd rather

buy jelly in a store like city people do. They never have to fool with fruit. And when they want a different kind, they just open a new jar. No neighbors sitting on the edge of every spoon.

"I'll finish the jars," Mama says. "You take the girls and get us some green tomatoes. Don't pick them all, though. Leave some to come ripe."

Taking the slat basket, off we go.

Afternoon only repeats morning. That's what gets me about Goose Rock. Except for school, the whole calendar is a hum. We put up chow-chow—that's corn and green tomato relish (Daddy's favorite); then the boys trudge in, heads hanging, clothes wilted; then there's supper—earlier because it's a week night and Daddy isn't here—then cleaning up, and sleep.

But I can't sleep. Anna wakes me up twice, muttering and thrashing. No words, but I suspect it's spider webs again. We're getting too big to sleep in one bed. Not enough room for bodies, much less dreams.

Footsteps cross the parlor; lamplight wavers. Is that Mama? I get up and tiptoe out to see.

Sure enough, she's sitting at her desk, Daddy's old shirt on over her gown. This is unusual. She always pays bills and writes to Omie Sunday night after Daddy leaves. I wait for her to know I'm there, wait while she writes a whole letter, but she's too intent to notice. Finally I just walk over.

"I couldn't sleep either," I say, by way of announcement.

She gives a start.

"Good gracious, Mandy, I didn't hear you at all."

"What are you doing?" Being the only other one awake makes me bold.

"Just business."

"With a jeweler?" I can see the envelope she's addressed: Ostriker's Jewelry in Memphis.

She studies me for a moment. "Well, Amanda, you are my oldest girl, so I guess I can tell you, but you must promise not to tell Daddy."

Not tell Daddy? We've never kept a secret from him. But still I nod.

"I'm ordering a ring."

"For Daddy?"

"No, no. A little emerald ring for me. You see, I haven't had anything pretty of my own in years—not since David was born. And every woman needs something pretty. It's like rain for the garden. Otherwise, she'll dry up and blow away."

But Mama, I want to say, look at that swollen belly. You're not exactly withering.

"Don't rings cost a lot?"

"Not always. Besides, fine jewelry is a good investment."

"I see," I say. "I guess I'll go back to bed."

"That's my girl."

I don't know. I look at her hard: rosy skin, brown hair fanned out around her face.

"Good night," I say, but I leave the room wondering why she gets a ring and I get leftover clothes.

6

 We've been in school a month now, and the weather turned gray as winter. But this morning, sunshine is back. Even the air glistens. David and Ben groan and stamp like horses on plowing day. Anna bounces:

> *School days, school days,*
> *Dear old golden rule days.*
> *Reading and writing and . . .*

"No singing at the table," Mama calls from the kitchen. "School will have started before you get out the door."

For some reason, she's decided Helen has to go to school with us too. Helen's only five and nobody likes the idea.

"I don't want to go," Helen whispers to me, a tear sliding right into her oatmeal.

"But you'll love it," I say, spooning brown sugar. "And Anna will be there."

"Where will you be?"

"I told you—I'll be right in the next room. And I'll see you when we go outside for lunch."

Helen's eyes widen.

"I have to stay with you or Mama."

"No, you don't. You'll be perfectly . . ."

"I have to!" Helen's voice climbs to a wail.

Mama fills the doorway.

"Well, for today Mandy can take you to Mr. Aden's room."

"I cannot!"

"Of course you can. It's just for one day."

"But it's not allowed."

"Amanda, don't tell me what's allowed. Today it's necessary." She bends down with difficulty, smoothing Helen's hair. "You boys get going. David, remember what I said."

"Yes, ma'am," he answers.

"It's not fair! It's bad enough that Helen has to go at all. She's not old enough. Miss Bledsoe won't want her. But for me to have to take her to Mr. Aden's room—"

Mama gives me a blazing look. "I don't want to hear any more about it. You'll do as you're told."

Someday I won't, I tell myself, jabbing at the oatmeal.

We set off up the road. Anna's still bouncing and Helen's pacified, but I feel robbed. What will Mr. Aden think when I come dragging in a five-year old? He'll think I have no respect for his classroom, that's what. And how can I pay attention with Helen pulling at my hand? She stops to look at a caterpillar measuring the road.

"Come *on*," I say, yanking at her braid. "The bell will ring and we'll still be in sight of home."

She looks up at me puzzled. Doesn't even say *ow*. But she gets moving.

"Please, Mr. Aden. It's only for today."

He takes a folded handkerchief from his coat pocket and blots his face. Harmon Wilson snickers.

"All right. But it's up to you to keep the child quiet."

Up to me! I smell tears starting and blink hard. She's not my child! But I nod.

And now I've displeased Mr. Aden. I glare at Helen as if that could stitch up her mouth.

She's good all morning, though, and dozes after lunch. We do Latin. I've forgotten a lot but I still like it. Roma Creech has forgotten it all and acts like it's Mr. Aden's fault.

"You didn't *teach* us *that*," she whines, her head bobbing.

Mr. Aden goes on. When he asks a question, Jimmy Halter rings out:

"Ain't no Latin in a coal mine."

Suddenly the sleepy room listens.

"Oh, but there is! Many of our everyday words come straight from Latin."

"Can't heat a house."

Irma giggles. Harmon winks at her across the aisle.

"The glow of knowledge has kept many a poor soul warm."

Low groans.

"I favor a fire," Jimmy drawls.

Mr. Aden comes down the row, hands behind his back.

"Mr. Halter," he begins, "do you know your way to the driftmouth?"

Half-laughs at this.

"If you mean Darby, up Burning Springs Road, I'd be a fool if I didn't."

"Then go right along and volunteer your services."

Jimmy just stares.

"They're not needed here."

A long pause. "Are you kicking me out?"

"No. But I'll oblige if you feel unable to walk."

This time the laughs are on Mr. Aden's side. Jimmy gets up and slinks toward the door.

"Now," Mr. Aden resumes, "the next sentence . . ."

Helen fairly dances on the way home.

"Your teacher threw a boy out of school! A big boy, bigger than Daddy."

"No, he's not."

"Sent him off to mine coal!"

Then she stops, her smile fading.

"Will Miss Bledsoe do that?"

"What?"

"If I can't read, will she send me down in the mine?"

"You silly!" Anna says. "Girls aren't allowed in coal mines. It's bad luck."

"But she might make me a checker or weigher."

That's what Mr. Skidmore does since he got hurt.

"Not until you can count."

"Anna, don't tease her. Miss Bledsoe won't send you out at all," I tell Helen. "Mr. Aden only did that today because Jimmy said coal mines were better than books."

"Are they?"

"Not for a minute."

"You can't eat books," Anna argues.

"You can't eat coal either."

"But you can sell coal."

Suddenly I realize how tired I am, how glad that we're almost home.

"The point is, Helen," I go on, "books give us something just as real as food or fire but we can't see it."

"Why not?"

"Can you see *that?*" Anna breaks in.

It's Mrs. Skidmore coming down the road.

"Mandy!" she calls. "Mandy!"

She looks strange without even one child in tow. But it's not just that. Her cheeks are flaming, her hair swarming out of its knot.

"You're not to go home," she declares, still ten feet away. "You're to bring the girls to my house."

"But why?"

By now she's square in front of me, hissing like a hot iron. "The baby's coming!"

"Are you sure?"

"Your mama sent David for Doc Bailey this morning, and Mr. Skidmore's gone after your daddy. Now come along. I left my babies."

She turns and huffs on down the road. Her blue-checked dress-tail snaps like a flag.

7

 So we spent last night at the Skidmores',
which could have been worse but mercifully
was not: a scrawny chicken red at the bone
for dinner, the littlest triplet spitting up in his plate.
Daddy had brought some quilts over, along with pick-
les and a basket of eggs. It was good to have something
of home to bed down on. And I fixed the eggs for
breakfast—just right.

We've hardly got started toward school when Daddy
runs up behind us.

"You have a little brother!" His face is so white it's
shining. "And Rena—your mother came through fine.
She's going to be just fine. You come on home after
school."

A brother! I'm astonished. I guess I assumed all the
ones after me would be girls.

"Now we are three of each," I tell Helen. "And *you*
are a big sister."

She takes a deep breath, swelling her dress front.

"Come right home," Daddy says again, turning back toward the house.

We've just crossed the creek bridge when I realize we don't have any lunch—Mrs. Skidmore didn't remember and neither did I. But it's not just the prospect of hunger which bothers me. It's something about Daddy insisting Mama will be fine. Of course she will. Why did he have to say that?

All day I worry. Even Mr. Aden sharing his cheese and fruit with us, eating lunch outside like a student, doesn't stop me. And now that we're walking home I feel like a rope in a tug-of-war. Part of me is pulled forward, around curves and right up the path to the house. The other part is tugged back to the schoolhouse, away from whatever's behind that door.

"What'll we name the baby?" Helen asks for the twentieth time.

"I don't know. Maybe *Jim* after Daddy."

"Or *Helen* after me."

"But you're a girl," Anna says. "Besides, you don't have two people in one family with the same name."

"Then how could they name him Jim?" Helen asks.

"She means two children," I explain. "They're going to *re*-name you Miss Question Box if you don't hush up."

Across the creek, around the big tulip poplar, and there's the house, same as always. Except Doc Bailey's buggy is tied up in front.

"What's he doing here?" Anna wants to know. "He already brought the baby."

The door is open, everything strangely still. And the glass on the door has been broken and boarded over.

"Mama?" I call. "Daddy?"

"Just a minute, Mandy," comes Daddy's voice. "Wait in the parlor."

We stop, barely inside the door.

Daddy comes through the dining room, even paler than this morning.

"Sit down," he says.

"I want to see the . . ."

"Not yet, honey." Something in his voice stops Helen.

We all sit on the couch, our sides touching.

"Your mother has had a bad time of it. She—she got into a bit of trouble today—Doc Bailey will explain it all when the boys get in—she's resting now, but she is real weak and needs quiet. For a long time she's going to need quiet. You girls can help me with that?"

We nod.

"Is the baby okay?" I have to ask. There's not a whimper in the house.

Daddy's face brightens. "Healthiest early baby you ever saw. Bigger than Helen was and she didn't come till she was ripe."

"What's his name?" Anna asks.

"Your mother wants to call him William."

"William?"

"After her brother who died. William Marion."

"Marion's a girl's name!" Anna protests.

"It was my father's," Daddy corrects her.

"William Marion Perritt: sounds awfully big for a baby."

"Amanda Virginia started out loose on you, too."

I hear David and Ben come into the yard. They didn't stay at the Skidmores', so they've already seen the baby, and come trooping into the house as usual. Then they see Daddy's face.

"What's wrong?" David begins.

"How come Doc Bailey's back?"

"Have a seat, boys. That's what we need to talk about. I'll see if Doc is ready now."

Ben eases into the rocker by the fireplace. David drops onto the couch.

"Babies cry," he declares. "That one in there cried all night."

"He's William," Anna ventures.

"He's *loud,*" David finishes up.

Daddy and Doc Bailey come out of the bedroom, collecting dining room chairs as they pass through. Then they sit in front of us, formal as church. I don't like this. It makes my stomach hurt.

"It's a good day and a bad day for you Perritts," Doc Bailey begins. Daddy clears his throat. "What I mean is, you have a big healthy brother, here to be a help and a credit to you all. But not quite yet. There's a lot to be done for this boy before you can send him out to hoe corn."

Daddy attempts to smile at this; David and Ben look like posts. Doc Bailey goes on:

"A baby takes a lot of raising, and a household takes a lot of running, and your mama is not going to be able to do much of either one for a while. She hemorrhaged—"

Daddy clears his throat again, looking from Doc Bailey to Anna and Helen.

"Women often do when babies are born, but this was an especially—an especially strong one, and she's lost a lot of blood. If she's to rebuild that blood and get her strength back, she's got to stay in bed, absolutely in bed, for six weeks."

Six weeks? Who will cook and do the wash and the sewing, not to mention take care of the baby? Who will take care of us?

"And after she's up," Daddy explains, "it will be a while before she can do what she used to. So we are all going to have to pitch in. We'll have to do things we've never done before. And do without some things we've always had. We'll have to take care of your mother, who's always taken care of us."

At this, Helen starts to cry.

"Now, Missy," Doc Bailey tells her, "you've got to be brave. But don't forget you have Mandy." He turns his watery blue eyes on me. "She's been a big help to her mother already. She won't let you go hungry and ragged, will you Mandy?"

I shake my head.

"Now, I have to be getting along. Alafair will have

supper waiting and I'll be in a stew myself if I don't get there to eat it. Haven't been home in three days."

Daddy walks him to the door. I remember the boarded-up hole.

"Who broke the door?" I ask when Daddy comes back.

"Maggie Skidmore. I'll tell you about that later. Right now I want to explain what we're going to do. For a while things will have to be very different—there's no way around it. I'll have to come home every night from the mill. Boys, it will be your job to keep the wash going. And with a baby that will be a lot of work. As for the fires, I'll do them in the morning and you can see that they're built up in the afternoon."

"Yes sir," Ben and David answer.

"Mandy, you'll be the cook."

"I can cook it if you can eat it," I say. Weak smiles all around.

"You little ones," he goes on, looking at Anna and Helen, "are not the littlest ones anymore, and you're going to have to do your share. Helen will keep going to school, and you'll both help around the house. We don't want it looking like a pigsty."

Solemn nods. He takes a deep breath.

"And Mandy," his eyes search my face, asking for something. "The only way to handle all this and the baby is for you to leave school for a while and take care of him."

I should have known this was coming, but I didn't. Tears knot up my throat and I can't speak. Daddy waits for a moment, then goes on:

"I know this is hard, Mandy, but it's not forever, and I see no other way to manage. I can't stay home and be a nursemaid. That's what you'll be, like Florence Nightingale."

I try to feel big-hearted. But Florence Nightingale didn't stay home, she didn't even stay in her own country. And school is the one thing I've got. I don't want to give that up. Willie's not my baby. I don't know how to take care of him and I don't want to either. It's not fair!

"You'll do that for me, won't you Mandy?"

Just then Willie cries, softly at first, then higher and louder with each breath. Daddy bolts for the bedroom. We sit silent, looking at the space he left.

In a minute he's back, carrying a bundle. Is there really a baby in all those blankets?

"Get up, son," he tells Ben. "Give Mandy the rocker."

We change places, like partners in a dance.

"Meet your brother," Daddy says. "One-day-old Willie Perritt." And bending over, he puts the baby in my arms.

8

A baby is a very heavy thing, any mother will tell you. Willie, settled in my arms, grew heavier than the house.

All month I've held him, bathed him, diapered him, carried him to and from Mama's breast. The little daylight he shuts his eyes to I spend working: meals, floors, Mama. I haven't crossed the creek or opened a book since Daddy put him in my lap.

I try to plan time for myself, but something always takes it. Like right now. The boys got behind on wash, so I've just finished a tubful of Willie's gowns. Had to string them up in front of the parlor fire since it's raining like Niagara Falls.

Now it's time to start peeling potatoes for dinner, and here come Anna and Helen from school. I hear them in the parlor. Why do they stand with the door open while they take off their coats? We can't heat the creekbed.

"Mandy!" Anna calls, the way I used to call "Mama!"

"I'm in the kitchen."

"Guess what!"

Anna dashes in, wet hair stringy, cheeks red.

"Miss Bledsoe says we can have a Christmas tree at school and we're each to bring an ornament. Vera Wilson gets to make the star, but Helen and I want to do angels. You've got to help us, though. We'll need—"

"Mine won't be an angel."

"Fancy cloth and tin foil and something soft for feathers—"

"Not mine."

"What did you say, Helen?"

Helen stands behind Anna, almost in the dining room.

"I don't want an angel. Mine is a wise camel."

"A what?"

"To follow the star."

"Oh, you mean a Wise Man's camel," Anna says, too loud, as though Helen can't hear.

There's a queer light behind Helen's head. I smell something too. O Lord! I almost knock the girls over getting to the parlor where Willie's gowns are blazing.

"Stay back!"

I reach for the afghan that's always on the couch. It takes forever to drag it through the air, but it smothers the flames. Awful smoke billows from the wool and the gowns.

"Open the door!" I call out to Anna, and as she does, the fire licks into the room. I might have thought of that, have known not to put them so close—

"Amanda!"

Now I've waked Mama.

"What's burning?"

I gather the mess in my arms, then drop it in the kitchen on the way to Mama.

She's propped up in bed, wearing the lacy bedjacket Omie sent her. She wasn't asleep, she was writing a letter, but her eyes are sleep-soft.

"It's all right," I tell her. "It was Willie's clothes. I had them drying in the parlor and they caught fire."

"Oh, Mandy!"

"I'm sorry. I should have thought—"

"Yes, you should. This house is a tinderbox. It could be gone in a minute."

Tears sting my eyes.

"Come here to me."

I take two steps toward the bed.

"Sit down."

I do that too, lifting my chin to try to keep the tears pooled.

"You've burned your hand."

Looking down spills the salt water. There's a crescent blister rising on the heel of my hand.

"Doesn't hurt."

"It will. Grease it good with butter."

I stand to go.

"And Mandy, I'm sorry I spoke so sharply. This is all too much for you. I need to get up and get to work."

"But you can't *do* that," I remind her. "For at least two more weeks you have to stay in bed. Don't worry. I'll be more careful. And I'll bring your strengthening pills."

Omie sent them along with the bedjacket. Mama

laughed when she read the label's claim to cure "fainting spells and a sense of goneness."

"I may be weak," she said, "but I certainly know I'm here."

I turn away from the bed. It doesn't matter if it's too much. I have to manage. . . .

Back in the kitchen, Anna asks, "Now what's Willie going to wear?"

Helen cuts in. "I *can* make a camel, can't I? Anna says they have to be angels, but angels only sing. The camels got across the desert."

"That's right, honey."

"And they brought the presents. The angels didn't bring a thing."

"They brought glad tidings."

"Not in a gold box."

"That's true."

"So you'll help me make a camel?"

"Sure."

"Right now?"

"Not right now. I have to work on supper. Besides, it's a long time till Christmas—"

"But camels are hard."

"Not as hard as angels," Anna taunts. "Angels have to look holy."

"Girls," I begin. But my peacemaking gets lost in Willie's cry.

9

That cry has gotten worse because Willie has colic. It's been going on about two weeks. He eats and falls asleep and then wakes up screaming. I've tried sugar water to burp him and a hot water bottle on his stomach, but nothing helps. Mama's had to quit feeding him in the night. If the cramps started then, he'd wake the whole house. The trouble is, the only way she can not feed him is if I walk him back to sleep. He won't take that from her, and anyway, she needs her rest. She's just been out of bed a few days.

So I never know how much I'll sleep. Last night it couldn't have been long. Willie woke three times. I walked him round and round the parlor, past midnight on the mountain, past the 3 A.M. train, past the sun coming into the hollow. I'd just fallen back to sleep when Daddy called us.

"You girls get up from there! You're wasting the best hours of the day."

Of course he didn't know how much I'd been up. He snores right through Willie's cries.

So up I got again, feeling half sick, and made biscuits and fried bacon and eggs.

David complained that the bacon was too hard. "Next time," I said, "you fix it for us." That hushed him.

I had hoped to go to church today, the first time since Willie, so I killed and plucked a chicken last night and put it in the icebox, ready for Mama to fry. But she was hardly out of bed when she told me, "Mandy, I'm afraid you'll need to stay home today. I've got that pain in my foot."

She hobbled into the kitchen and did a few dishes, but before long she had to go sit down. The pain comes because her heart was damaged. She doesn't get enough blood to her legs.

I try not to cry, looking at the breakfast leavings. I can't really say God was calling me to church. I just wanted a wintry ride in the wagon and a chance to see a face or two from school. Even breathing other air is good for a body. And instead I'm left with a pile of dirty plates. That's not so much, but in a few hours there'll be dinner, and the dishrag hardly dry before supper comes on.

Another hope I had was to do some schoolwork. Last week Mr. Aden sent me a book, *The Romantic Poets*. His note said if I'd read it and write a piece about it, that would fulfill my English requirement. I was thrilled.

But I haven't had a chance to open it. For one thing, I've had to help Anna and Helen with their ornaments.

Anna was scornful when I suggested tin-foil angel wings.

"Tin-foil doesn't look holy!" she said. "And we've got plenty of feathers."

We do, but chicken feathers are too small to paste. I found that out the hard way, with Anna mad and half feathered herself. We had to take some goose down from one of our pillows.

"Don't tell Mama," I cautioned.

"Is this stealing?" Helen wanted to know.

"I don't think so. Anyway, you can't go to jail for stealing feathers for angel wings."

The camel was tricky too. Felt wouldn't do for his fur.

"He should feel rough," Helen insisted.

We tried sawdust, but that was as messy as feathers. Finally I sent her outside for some sandstone. Our mountain is good for that. It's limestone on the Laurel County side and sandstone on ours.

We cut another camel shape from a cardboard box, spread it with paste and rolled it in sand rubbed off the rock. It dried and sparkled.

"He's made of desert!" Helen exclaimed. Then she pasted yarn on for a saddle and we were done.

But by then Anna had a quarrel about her angel.

"I don't like her mouth. It's silly. And angel eyes are blue, not brown."

So we made another face and glued that on. When will it get better? Mama can only do a little and most of that is for Willie.

The first thing she wanted to do when she got up

was give him his bath. That made me sad. I would abandon the kitchen in a minute, but I miss that bath. Willie loves water. No matter how he has fussed, a tubful soothes him, and if he's been happy, he smacks the water and laughs. Daddy says he's too young to be laughing, but that's what he's doing. And I laugh with him.

If I'm going to get this dinner ready, I'll have to wash the dishes, so I dip hot water from the reservoir built into the stove. Then I take the chicken from the icebox and lay it out to dry. Mama says if chicken is wet in the least it won't fry right. I know all about chicken.

What I don't know is when I can go back to school. Should I ask? I puzzle over this washing dishes, frying chicken, putting the big kettle of potatoes on to boil. And then I hear Daddy coming in the door.

"Smell that chicken!" he calls out to the boys. "I wonder if that could be your Mama's."

"Not this time," she answers. "I'm still peg-legging around. How was the service?"

The familiar pattern of their voices drifts to the kitchen. Anna's drowns it out.

"Look what I've brought you, Mandy! Daddy said I could."

She careens around the dinner table, Helen behind her. They each hold a bunch of bittersweet.

"Where did you get it?" I ask, accepting the swatch of orange berries.

"They had it left over from decorating the church," Anna explains.

"And I brought some for Mama," Helen says.

"Good for you."

"I wanted to give it to you, but Anna wouldn't let me. She said Mama ought to have some."

"She's right. You run along and give it to her."

Helen goes. I turn back to the chicken, the green beans. Anna makes no move to put her coat up.

"How was church?"

"Fine. Miss Snavely asked about you."

"What did you tell her?"

"I said you were pining to go back to school."

"Really?"

I don't know whether I'm more amazed that Anna knew this or mad that she said it.

"And what did Miss Snavely say?"

"Said that was a lot of foolishness, that you were getting the best education a girl could have."

I don't answer that.

"She said you were lucky, learning all you are now."

"Well, she's wrong," I snap. "You are the lucky ones, and don't you forget it. You and Helen and the boys."

"Going to school? What's lucky about that? I'd rather stay home like you and play with Willie."

"You don't know what you're talking about, Anna."

Suddenly Mama comes in.

"Anna, you hang your coat up. And help Helen."

When they're gone, she says, "That's no way to talk to your sister."

"But it's the truth."

"According to Amanda Perritt. That doesn't mean gospel."

There's almost a laugh in her voice. I let out a deep breath. I don't talk back. But I mash the potatoes with a vengeance.

Soon we are all seated at the table. I take my old place at the side to make room for Mama. Daddy blesses us and sends around the food. The gravy I made isn't as good as Mama's, but it covers. I eat it all off the crown of my potatoes and ask for more. Mama looks at me and the boys and then at Daddy, measuring.

"I think not, Mandy," she says. "You don't want to get plump like me."

That's not what she means and she knows it. My ribs stick out. She means, leave it for your brothers, your daddy. Never mind if you want some more. And I made it!

David's hand edges toward the gravy boat.

All of a sudden I feel fire like Willie's gowns blazing. It's all around me. If I stay in my seat, if David's hand touches the china, I'll be caught in a roar of flames. So I grab the gilt-edged handle, stand up, and hurl the gravy boat at the wall.

It sails over David's head and smashes and the fire I felt is a fierce joy. Let them stare! Let the china splinter in the rug and the gravy run down the wall.

10

Everyone at the table seems to hold his breath while I go to the kitchen for a rag and a bowl. Gradually, as I wipe gravy from the wallpaper and pick china fragments from the rug, they resume talking, but nobody says a word about what's happened. Anna and Helen must be biting their tongues. When I finish, I come back to my place and dig meat off the back of the chicken. I did take the back. Mama will have to give me credit for that.

All the time I'm clearing the table and washing up I'm waiting for her anger. There's nothing. When Willie wakes, she disappears into the bedroom. Even Anna and Helen steer clear, and the boys have gone to hunt squirrel in the bare trees. I feel invisible. Is that what happens when you let your feelings out? No one can see you?

Well, if that is the way of things, I can take it. I just wish I'd thrown something which didn't break. Or didn't match. We don't have many dishes that do.

The kitchen is done and the house is still as midnight. I take Mr. Aden's book and sit down to read.

Tuesday now and still no mention of the gravy boat. Mama's stronger, doing a little more each day. And she studies me on the sly whatever we're doing. I catch her at it. Does she want to get out of the way in case I throw something else?

Right now Doc Bailey's here to look at Willie.

"This boy's not sick," he says. "Just immature digestion."

But Mama worries. "I'm afraid it's because I've neglected him."

"Hogwash!" Doc Bailey tells her. "He'd have colic if you'd been sitting by him day and night. I'll give you some syrup to soothe him. You don't have any business being up all hours."

"It's Mandy who gets up."

"Or Mandy either." He turns to me. "You're getting your motherhood early." The way he says it makes it sound like something I could wear.

He opens his worn bag, with its shelves of pills and liquids, and pulls out a bottle of something green as grass.

"This should do the trick." He hands it to Mama. "Let me know and I'll write a prescription if you need more."

We thank him, feeling a little shamefaced since Willie has been quiet as an egg ever since he came. Just smiled and waved his hands when the doctor felt his belly.

"That's the way it goes," Mama says after Doc Bailey is gone. "Five minutes with a doctor can cure a child—till the doctor leaves."

And she's right. Willie wails again as soon as she feeds him, knees drawn up, face tight as a fist. And we can't give him the medicine till bedtime. But when we do, it works like a charm. For me that means the first real sleep since the Skidmores'.

I wake up before dawn in a panic. Willie! I run into Mama's room, my heart loud as thunder. The tiny back under the crib quilt rises and falls. Mama is a big ball in bed. And I am as awake as I'll ever be. Feeling foolish, I put on the coffee and take up the book.

> *Now, while the birds thus sing a joyous song,*
> *And while the young lambs bound*
> *As to the tabor's sound,*
> *To me alone there came a thought of grief . . .*

It isn't ten minutes till Willie cries. I go in as usual to change him before giving him to Mama, but she's already up, crooning to him.

"This boy slept all night!" she proclaims, happy as Christmas. Willie stares at her face like a great light.

I try to be glad. I *am* glad about the sleeping, but I feel useless. I thought it was *me* Willie needed.

"We're fine here," Mama says. "You start breakfast."

Anybody'd rather hold a baby than cook.

The rest of the day and the week are like that, too: Mama gaining strength and taking over. Not enough for me to go to school, but enough to talk about it. Yet no one does. Is that my punishment?

It's Friday night now, and Mama and Daddy are figuring. Given all that's happened with Willie, I'd forgotten about the mill, forgotten to worry. Tonight Helen asks Daddy about the big ledger book.

"You're doing your books," she says. "What are you studying?"

"How money disappears."

"Are you a scholar?"

"No, honey. Just a Professor of Hard Times."

She stares at him.

"I wish I were a scholar," he says. "It's going to take some research to figure out how to make ends meet."

Mama signals for us to go to our room.

Once down the hall, Helen continues her questions.

"Ends of what?"

"He means we're poor," Anna offers.

"The whole country is poor right now, not just Perritts."

"Who's going to meet their end?"

"No, no, that's not what he's talking about. He means making the money which comes in equal the money that goes out. Having a balance."

"How can he do that?"

"Well, I'm not sure. It takes adjustments."

"Oh. Do we have some?"

"You don't have adjustments; you make them."

"Could we make some?"

"We already have. We've adjusted a lot to Willie's coming."

"But that didn't have to do with money," Anna puts in.

I think about that.

"Well, it did in a way. If I hadn't stayed home, we would have had to hire help to look after Willie and Mama."

"So you kept money from going out?"

"Sort of."

"Like the boy at the dike."

"What?"

"That's a story we heard at school," Anna explains. "But he was keeping the water *out*, Helen, out of the village."

"And *in* the sea," Helen insists. "Like the money. Mandy's been keeping the money *in*."

I wish I'd thought of that. Somehow it makes me feel a lot better.

"You girls get ready for bed," Mama calls.

I start to help Helen out of her dress.

"I can do it myself now," she says. "Since Willie, my arms are longer."

Mine, too, I guess. But I hadn't even noticed I'd quit helping her. Why didn't Anna do it?

Anna's got her dress off, her gown on, and has jumped into bed.

"Anna, get up and brush your hair. And your teeth."

"I'm too tired."

"No, you're not."

"Your teeth will fall out and get stuck in your hair," Helen warns.

You can tell she's been to school.

Anna rolls out of bed and does what's needed. We're all about settled when Mama appears at the door.

"Come into the kitchen a minute, Amanda."

I climb out of the warm bed, stone cold. I half expect to see every china chip laid out on the table, a note written in blood beside it: You must put it back together by morning or die.

But this isn't a fairy tale. Daddy is seated at the work table drinking coffee. Mama motions me to have a seat.

"Mandy," Daddy begins—he never calls me Amanda, no matter how serious things get—"your mother and I appreciate all your work since Willie came. We know it's not been easy. You're the only child I've got who would grieve missing school, and you're the one who's had to do it. . . ."

He pauses and Mama goes on.

"So now that I'm better—"

"You mean I can go back to school?"

I blurt this out from excitement and relief.

"After Christmas, yes," Mama continues, "but before that we have a present for you."

A present? The first thing I think of is the ring Mama ordered. It seems years ago and I'd forgotten all about it. But I don't want a ring, not with money like it is.

"You like trains, don't you?" Daddy says, as if to fill up the silence.

"Sure." But they can't be going to give me a toy

train. I don't know what to do. They're both looking at me.

"Omie's invited you to come to Memphis," Mama says. "It's your Christmas present. And we'd like to let you go."

I can't believe it.

"You mean on the train?"

Daddy nods.

"By myself?"

It's all I can do to keep from saying: Without Willie?

"Just you," Mama confirms. "A week and a half to visit and see the sights."

"And describe that baby to your grandmother," Daddy adds. "She wants an eye-witness."

I smile. "Are you sure it's all right? I mean . . ."

"Well, we wouldn't be ready to spare you tomorrow," Mama admits. "But I'm stronger every day, and in another week—"

"But I'll be there at Christmas!"

"That's right," Daddy says. "You can ride streetcars hung with holly."

"And eat Mama's plum pudding."

And miss yours, I think. And miss Willie looking at the tree.

"I don't think she wants to go," Daddy says to Mama.

"Yes I do! I just can't believe it, that's all."

"Well, it's settled. You go on to bed, and we'll talk tomorrow."

"I don't think I can sleep."

"Want a spoon of Willie's potion?" Daddy offers.

"Jim!" Mama's shock is half real. "Sit still then, Mandy. I'll make you some cocoa."

And that's the strangest thing of all: sitting at the table while Mama waits on me, a huge gift where I'd expected a slap in the face.

11

Before Helen was born, we used to go to Memphis once a year. "Come summer, I have to go home," Mama would say, and pack a trunk and a hamper. I only remember the last two visits: red waxy flowers in Omie's back yard, Aunt Laura pretty as a catalogue cover, Opie peeling apples with his pocket knife. One trip the boys disappeared the moment the train pulled out and Mama told me to quit looking out the window and watch Anna till she found them.

But it won't be like that this time. I'll be on my own. I close my eyes and see myself sitting on the red plush seat, brave and lonely.

Maybe I'll feel I belong in Memphis. It's a real city, even if it's not Boston. Things happen there—interesting things to interesting people. I've seen that in Aunt Laura's eyes.

Mama said I can go a week from Sunday. That's tomorrow. Ben and David took no notice, even when she told David he might go down next summer to work for Opie.

"If I'm going to saw logs, I might as well saw them here," was all he said. He doesn't want to leave Polly.

Mama told the girls, too. Anna was mad.

"Mandy gets to do everything! Stay out of school to take care of Willie! Go see Omie and Opie! It's not fair."

But Helen got tearful.

"What if you forget how to come back?"

I explained about the railroad, the track being nailed down and going both ways. And about a round-trip ticket.

"But if it's round, you don't come back like you went. That's straight."

"Helen—" I always forget she sees each word-picture. You have to tell her it's not real.

"Round trip just means the ticket will bring you back."

I told Willie I'm going. He smiled with his lips tucked in. That's his new trick. He practices all the time. Last week he worked on his tongue. Not sticking it out, but smiling with it laid from his lip to his chin. He's never idle. If he's not asleep, he's nursing, working, or crying. I admire him. He knows he's got a lot to do and he doesn't waste a minute.

I wonder if he'll know I'm gone. Will he forget me? Mama says he won't, but the idea makes me sad. In two weeks he'll be a different baby. Mama's baby.

I don't see how I can feel so many things. I want

to go—of course I do. I'm ready as a big red tomato is to get off the vine. Then why does the vine suddenly seem fragile, like it might wither up if I'm gone? No, that's not right. I'm more afraid the vine doesn't need me, will grow right over the place where I was. Before Mama got better it felt like I *was* the vine. Now I don't know.

And last week, when the Christmas box came from Omie and Opie, I felt left out because there wasn't a present for me. Isn't that silly, when mine is the biggest gift of all?

What with packing and fretting the week has spun by. It's a cold Saturday night and we're loaded in the wagon to go to the train. I can tell David and Ben are sour about being here. They had to get their chores done early. But Mama insisted that the whole family take me.

It's a squeeze to get us all in. Anna sits up with Mama. I'm back with the boys, and Helen sleepy in my lap. I was hoping to hold Willie but Mama didn't offer. Anyway, Helen seems rooted. She's the only one somber to see me go.

Daddy coaxes Midge and Welkie and we start rolling, between mountains that stand like a deeper part of the dark. The only sound besides the wagon's rattle is Mama singing:

> *O, the moon shines tonight on pretty Red Wing.*
> *The breeze is sighing, the nightbirds crying.*

Far, O far beneath the stars her brave is sleeping
While Red Wing's weeping her heart away.

Willie's wrapped in sleep and song and quilts.

We come to the wagon bridge. Daddy eases us on it. There's no rail; he has to have dead aim. He carries a lantern, of course, but its glow doesn't go far, and there's not much moonlight. We travel the road by heart.

A little ways downcreek from the wagon bridge is the footbridge—just two logs, fun to balance across. But there was one time I couldn't make it. In the rattly silence it comes back to me, that hard day I was coming home.

I was seven maybe, seven or eight. It was early winter and we'd just moved to Goose Rock. I'd waked up that morning feeling jumbled, like the inside me had come loose from my bones. My back ached and I was hot, but Mama couldn't feel it, so off I went with David and Ben to school.

I did all right through the morning, but by lunch my feet rose over my shoes like bread. I told Miss Bledsoe.

"You're hot as blazes," she said. "Get your coat and go straight home."

I didn't think to question, just put books in my satchel and headed out. The wool of my red coat smelled funny. Somehow I thought I could smell that it had grown too red. And my eyes didn't go where they should.

But I walked. Like Welkie and Midge in this darkness, I knew the road, and I trusted it to pull me. But as I got heavier, it had to tug harder, and when I topped the hill above Goose Creek I realized I was too big for the footbridge; I'd have to cross like a wagon. Then when I reached the rough lip of that bridge, I couldn't stand up. My feet had ballooned. I got down on all fours, grateful for knees. The bridge appeared to me a long ladder. I had to haul myself up as well as across. But I made it. And crawled the rest of the snow-crusted way home.

Anna was the baby then. Mama came to the door with her wrapped in a shawl. She didn't see me at first, then she screamed. I couldn't speak for the heat rushing out the door.

I don't remember much about the next few days. I know Doc Bailey came, bringing shots and little envelopes of big pills. And Mama's face kept appearing above me, like the moon tonight. "I see the moon and the moon sees me. . . . " Did she sing that?

And why does this come back now? Is it the cold? Is it Anna in my made-over coat? Mama has given it a black velvet collar and pocket. This didn't impress Anna, but Helen was thrilled.

"Your pocket has a coat!" she said, over and over. "I want a pocket with a coat."

"It will come to you," Mama promised. "Anna is just one stop on this little coat's road."

"Where is it going?"

"Probably to a rug."

Omie braids rugs out of our old clothes—"anything that's got body but no spirit left." The parlor rug is mostly David and Daddy, the dining room, David and Ben and me. So that, too, will be cut and stitched and twisted, the too-red coat that belonged to a pocket, the Mandy-Anna-Helen coat. Willie won't need it.

Helen has just fallen asleep and we're rolling into Manchester. There's the Lyttle house: white, three stories, with a windowed turret. Daddy once said we'd live there when our ship came in.

"When will that be?" David wanted to know.

All Daddy said was, "Don't know as I've ever seen a ship in these mountains."

At the train station Mama insists that everybody get out.

"We must see Mandy off in style."

Style is hardly the word for all the bodies spilling from the wagon. David carries my bag and Ben brings the present box. Then Daddy hands me the ticket, Mama straightens my coat, everybody gives me a kiss, and I climb into the train. After the long ride, this part happens too fast. I don't even ask to hold Willie.

When I find my seat I look out the window. There they stand: Daddy behind Mama, his hands on her shoulders; the boys straight and thin, trying not to kick stones; Anna lifting her dress to look at the lace on her petticoat, and Helen's face wet as if she'd stood in the rain. She must have hurt herself, I think. But no, she's waving and searching for me. And then I realize that they all look sad, like a field when the sun has just left it. I try to see if Willie is crying, but Mama has him on her shoulder.

And here I am on board, the seat solid oak and red plush, the windows filmed with dust. Beside me is the supper that Mama has packed—fried chicken and a piece of jam cake; in my lap is a book and handkerchief and money Daddy gave me for the trip. I'm all set for an elegant journey. But a man sits across the aisle, his cheek pouched with tobacco, and every few minutes he spits into a can.

12

The train has a hard time leaving. It jerks and strains and shakes. I feel that way too.

If anyone had told me a month ago that I'd be sad to leave home, I would have scorned them like Miss Snavely. But I am sad.

I remember what I told Helen: the nailed-down track is connected—Goose Rock to Memphis—and will bring me back. I'm grateful for that.

I wonder how Mr. Aden felt coming to Goose Rock, leaving behind the paved world he knew. But Mr. Aden is a grown-up and a man: why should he worry? Men always know what to do. Turn some kind of labor into money. So he came to teach. And to live. Volunteered to eat fatback and breathe coal dust. I'll never understand it.

Mama let me walk to school Friday afternoon to tell him about my trip.

"What a splendid chance for you!" he said. He always has these silky words like splendid. "What will you do?"

"See my kin, mostly," I told him.

"But you must see Memphis, too. It's the place to take the pulse of the Mississippi, to follow the Old South's shadows."

"Yes sir," I answered, trying to sound like I knew what he was talking about.

Later I asked Mama. She smiled her Mr. Aden smile. I felt silly.

"Well, Memphis *is* on the river and that's made it important in trade—cotton and lumber—that's probably what he means. Opie can take you to his mill, if that would please you. . . ."

I nodded, but I knew Mr. Aden didn't mean sawdust. I've seen plenty of that in Goose Rock. Maybe I'll ask Aunt Laura.

After a while I unpack a drumstick but can't eat it. The train makes me woozy. Then I fall asleep and wake up starving. Mama says it's lucky that I like dark meat, since you often have to leave the white pieces for guests. She means for men, though she doesn't say it. I think about this, chewing chicken, watching the lights out the window.

When the news butch comes through, I ask for a cream soda. What catches my eye on his tray, though, is clear glass bottles, shaped like train engines and filled with bits of candy. They're small enough to fit in the palm of your hand.

At Chattanooga a woman gets on with a baby smaller than Willie, so swaddled you can't see its face. She takes a seat somewhere behind me, and I hear the baby's gurgle, her low response. They make me feel cold all at once and empty. I wrap up in my coat and try to count the stars.

"Count all the stars," Daddy says, "and you'll never be forgotten."

One day I plan to ask him what that means.

Sometime in the night I wake up and eat the jam cake. The heavy sweetness sets me to thinking about the day we picked the berries.

It was late July. Anna and Helen and I went out early, hoping to beat both the bees and the heat. We did for a while; then Anna closed her hand on a berry so plump she didn't see the bee. She shrieked. Mama had made me bring a wet-rag-and-soda poultice. I used that and we went on picking.

I could tell when it neared noon and we ought to be quitting, but Anna's hand was okay and there were two bushes to go.

"I have a halo," Helen declared.

"That's good," I told her. "You're the world's first blackberry angel."

"You can feel it."

"Yep," I said, my purple hand grazing her hair.

"Blackberries can see it," she insisted. "That's why they're winking."

And she tumbled, halo first, into the bush.

Before she'd come to rest, I knew what had happened: sunstroke. Stupid, stupid, my heart thumped with every step I took up the meadow, Helen on my shoulder, Anna carrying the buckets.

Once inside, I could see Helen's red scalp. Mama cooled her down while Anna and I rinsed berries. She came to right away.

"Mandy said I was a blackberry angel."

"Well," Mama cautioned, "don't fly away just yet." She gave me a look, steep as any scolding.

"I'm sorry. I should have realized."

"Yes, you should. Heatstroke is dangerous, especially for a little child."

"I said I'm sorry."

"Ten more minutes might have made you a good deal sorrier."

The truth of that settled in through the afternoon. Helen rested. We made jam and a big cobbler.

"Pie supper tonight," Mama announced.

Pie suppers are how we celebrate birthdays in summer—thick berry juice laced with strips of crust. Daddy can't eat the seeds, so Mama strains out the berries. This one was for David, who turned sixteen that week.

Ben teased him. "I guess you'll run off and marry Polly now."

David didn't even blush. "Mandy's almost twelve. I'll leave the courting to her."

"You will not!" My cheeks felt as red as Helen's scalp.

"Just wait till next year. Some tall fellow will show up and put your heart in his pocket."

Ben added, "If he can get her notice over the rim of a book."

Daddy saw me steaming.

"That's enough, boys."

Little did we know I'd get a baby long before a sweetheart. Or eat those berries rocked in the cradle of a train.

13

 A night's train ride and the world has changed: flat red earth, big fields, patches of pine trees. I look out the window and consider the people I'm going to meet.

Mama says mountain people are different from southerners and Delta people are different even from that. Then Daddy says, "Are you sure it's not just your people who are different?" She has kin over in the Delta.

But I'm not going to the Delta. I'm headed for Memphis, with its big white sorrowful houses and voices soft as flour. "Sorrowful houses" is my grandmother Omie's description. One of my favorite things about her is how she says things that sound like a book. I remember what she wrote when she heard about Willie, and Mama's sickness after his birth: "That child, that child. A cup of sunshine in a tub of rain." And of course she was right.

Omie knows all about babies. She had three by her first husband, Mama's daddy, Mr. Grace. After he died, she married Opie and had four more. Mama was her oldest girl—like me. You know, I never thought of that. She probably had to help Omie a lot, too. There was her little sister Edith, who died, and then a half brother and three half sisters. One of those is my Aunt Laura, who sent me her clothes.

Omie says Laura is her hothouse flower, "though how she took root in a coffee-ground garden I don't know."

Don't let that fool you. Omie's garden is perfect; her flowers come up bouquets. It's true she mixes coffee grounds in her flowerbed, but that's for a purpose. Mama does it too.

"It lightens the soil," say Omie and Mama.

Daddy claims they have the only daylilies open to the moon.

"They've got the big eye," he says.

But Aunt Laura is different. She doesn't push your hair back and say you've grown. She doesn't cook. She's married, to Uncle Cresswell, but she doesn't have any children.

"Imagine a baby spitting up on my shantung dress!" she said one summer when we were visiting.

"If you had babies you wouldn't be wearing silk dresses," Mama told her.

"That's what I know," said Aunt Laura.

And she doesn't keep house. She doesn't even always live in one. For a while she and Uncle Cresswell stayed in the Hotel Emory, so they could "be near the center of things," they said. Could walk to the theater, the symphony, the ballet.

"My stars and time," said Omie. "The center of things is the kitchen and the cradle, and I don't know how I raised a girl who doesn't know that."

"Different people have different centers," said Aunt Laura.

That's so true I'd like to print it in the paper.

Anyway, now Aunt Laura and Uncle Cress live in a house on Catalpa Street. But that doesn't mean Aunt Laura breaks her nails scrubbing laundry and baseboards. She has servants. And servants are not the same as Help. Mama had Help after Helen was born, a poor girl from up on Big Goose. Stayed with us a month, doing wash and looking hungry, her eyes as dull as a dry creek stone. Help is somebody you know you're helping too. Servants are trained. They don't eat with you.

So I am looking forward to seeing Aunt Laura. Maybe I can tell her how I feel about different centers. And how I don't want babies. How I didn't sprout up in the coffee-ground garden either. Maybe she will take me to the theater. She can drive a motor car herself, you know. Maybe she'll take me for a ride. Maybe she'll even let me sit behind the wheel.

14

 As we pull into Union Station, I see Omie and Opie waiting, as much a pair as bookends. Their clothes aren't alike, Opie's gray coat and Omie's rose, but they stand close and their faces look for the same thing.

Me.

All of a sudden, I feel shy, backward. My going-away dress Mama was so proud of looks dull and homely. My hair hangs limp, like someone cut it in the kitchen, which Mama did.

But Omie and Opie don't seem to notice.

"She's grown a mile!" Opie exclaims, giving me a hug. "She'll outstrip her mother in no time."

"Let me see your hands, child," Omie says, putting her gloved hand palm to palm with mine. "Heavens, yes. Your hands are already larger than Rena's. You must take after me."

Omie is tall, and draws herself up as she says this.

Mama calls her "Tall and handsome."

Daddy always adds, "Like a sailing ship."

We ride home in Opie's car—black with curtains and a bud vase. There's a rosebud in it, pink and tight as a baby's fist. When we get to the house on Poplar, Omie sends me up to bathe while she finishes Sunday dinner.

Like magic, hot water comes out of a pipe into the huge cold tub. I'm used to bathing in a washtub in the kitchen in shared water. I can't believe all this luxury is for me. I take off my clothes and slide in, like a spoon in a big sauce boat, and lie back and close my eyes. There's a wonderful smell of enamel and rose-water soap drifting over the soothing sway of the bath. It's like the train only quiet and sweet smelling. Like the train . . .

"Dinnertime, Mandy!"

I must have been asleep! The water is cool and I haven't even washed. I do my face and hands and feet and climb out quickly. It wouldn't do to keep them waiting.

Omie's table is not just set, it's arranged. Everything has a special dish and they all match. I set myself down slowly, not wanting to break even the silence.

But of course Omie and Opie want to hear all about home—Omie asking about Mama and the babies, and Opie asking about Daddy and the mill. And the lads, as he calls David and Ben.

"Do they know their wood?" he asks me. "Can they walk a boundary of timber?"

The truth is, I don't know whether they can or not.

"They can wash clothes," I tell him.

"Wash clothes!" he rumbles.

Opie never thunders, but he lets on like he might. His eyes are gray and what hair he has is white and stands out like lightning. He's just a little taller than Omie, and portly.

"Yes, wash clothes," answers Omie. I can't answer. My mouth is full. "Rena has been sick you will remember." Then she says she's proud of how we all managed. "Especially you, Mandy," she says, reaching for my hand. "Your mama told me you helped with the house and the baby like you'd been doing it all your life."

Not exactly, I want to say, remembering the time I set Willie's clothes on fire; and the time I served spoiled meat, not recognizing the smell; and the time I tried to make cookies with leftover oatmeal. Not exactly. But I just smile.

"You'll be that much ahead when you're a wife and mother yourself," Omie goes on. "A baby won't be a jolt to you."

No indeed, I think, because I won't have one. But I don't say that. I butter the roll I've lifted from Omie's silver basket. It's light as a baby's breath.

After dinner and dishes, we sit at a card table in the living room playing Rummy. There's never time to play cards at home—too many bodies to look after. I'm just about to say this when Opie says, "Remember how Rena loved to play bridge? I never knew a soul better at it. She could beat us all when she'd been playing only two weeks."

That's a surprise. I've never seen Mama play cards.

"Of course, she played wild," Opie continues.

"Wanted to take the bid regardless of her cards. But her bluff was sufficient."

That sounds even less like Mama.

"And as soon as you realized that," Omie says, "you made her your partner. That meant you both were going to win."

"Have to look out for your prospects," Opie answers, sweeping up the cards to shuffle. "Can't do millwork if you don't know the grain of the wood."

"Honestly," Omie sighs. "The world to your granddaddy is an oak tree and a buzz saw."

"And Jim Perritt's the same," Opie counters. "And Rena's is rinse water and a coconut cake."

"That shows what you know about women's work," Omie tells him. "You're like a child trying to sound the Mississippi with his school ruler."

She winks at me.

I've thought about that ever since I got in bed. Omie means it to seal the secrets that we share, woman secrets. But I'm not sure we share them. I think I might choose the ruler and the river. I think I'd like to let myself down into something too big to measure. Cake pans and wash kettles are just too small for me.

15

Waking up in Memphis is not at all like waking up in Goose Rock. The sun doesn't have to strain to get over mountains; the air is rich and flat. It's not just the wide paved streets but the river—everything feels light and free, like the day you peel off your winter underwear.

Opie has left for the mill by the time I get downstairs, but there are eggs and biscuits in the warming oven.

"I'll have another cup of coffee while you eat," Omie says. "Would you like some?"

"I'd like to try. Mama doesn't allow me coffee at home."

"Don't that beat all!" Omie says, smiling. "Rena was drinking coffee when she was half your size. You can tell her I said that."

As I watch Omie pour the dark drink into a flowered cup, I realize it's not age that keeps me from getting coffee at home, it's money. Surely Omie knows that. She sets the cup by my plate.

"Today," she declares, "Opie brings home our

Christmas tree. He's had his eye on it all fall and just dug it up last week."

"Dug it up?"

"Oh yes. You'd think a man who makes a living cutting trees wouldn't blink at chopping down one more for Christmas. Not Opie. He'll drag this fellow home, tend it like a babe, and then take it back to the woods."

"You couldn't do that at home," I say, thinking out loud. "The ground would be frozen."

"That rarely happens here. Anyway, Opie says this one's big enough for all our decorations, so this morning you and I need to get them out."

After breakfast she carries in two big boxes.

"Opie got these down from the attic before he left."

Mama says we're never sure of staying anywhere long enough to put things in the attic. Our tree tinsel is all in Mama and Daddy's chifforobe.

Omie's decorations are wrapped in tissue: red candleholders, a string of silver beads. There are a few wooden ornaments—a dog, a piano—and red and green glass balls. Finally, at the bottom of the second box, the star—peeling silver with a bent green outline.

"I know it's shabby," Omie says, slipping her finger into the spring which holds the star to the treetop, "but William got it for me, that first Christmas after the war. He was our oldest child, you know, Opie's and mine. He was your mother's half brother, but he might as well have been her son the way she doted on him. And when he came home from France without a scratch—we could hardly breathe, we were that happy. Met him at Union Station, same as you. All those uniforms, some boys wounded, crippled, and ours straight and whole as the finest tree. We cried then, I'm telling you, even Opie, and Rena had her arm through William's all the way home."

Omie looks at me, but it's not me she's seeing. Maybe not anybody.

"Well, we'd heard, of course, of the flu epidemic. And I worried some. But I guess I figured William was charmed. He looked the part: deep blue eyes, hair dark as poplar honey. And even when he took sick, he joked and carried on.

" 'Send me the prettiest nurses! And send Rena! She's better than a flower cart.'

"Two weeks in bed, the fever broke and he began eating. Before you knew it he was up walking around. Got me this star from Ostriker's Jewelry, went with Opie to the mill."

"Did he get the flu again?"

"No, no, it wasn't that."

She slips the star off and lays it on the table.

"By Christmas week, William was his old self. Going to dances, helping bring home the tree. But the flu had done something to his heart. New Year's Day it stopped while he was shaving. A boy who survived the battlefields. Who would believe it?"

"I'm sorry," I say.

Omie shakes her head.

"It was a long time ago."

"But you remember."

"Oh, honey, I remember when the midwife put him in my arms."

"Like Willie."

"We never called him Willie."

"I mean our Willie—like Daddy handing him to me."

"How old is that baby?"

"Almost three months."

"William was twenty-one. And Rena—the way it took her, well I thought we might lose her too. That's what happened to the star."

"What?"

"We didn't put Christmas away until after the funeral, and Rena and I were right in this room taking down the tree. I slipped this from the top branch and it sent the needles raining. 'William's star,' I said as I handed it down.

"Your mother tried to tear it apart and, when that didn't work, she threw it across the room."

Mama?

" 'I never want to see another Christmas,' she said, over and over. When I went to fetch the star, she called it stupid, ugly. 'Why should it last and William be gone?'

"No answer to that, of course, but I'm glad to have it."

She holds up the battered star.

"William knew quality. And this was his gift. I'll bet Rena wouldn't scorn it now."

* * *

Opie brings the tree—a soft-needled pine—and after lunch we set it up on the little sun porch. Clip on the candleholders, drape the beads, and set the star. When I reach for a glass ball, Omie says, "I used to save that part for Laura."

"You mean for her tree?"

"No, to put on ours. She never has one of her own."

"Why not?" I blurt out.

"It's Cress partly. He says plants and animals belong outside. And he and Laura move so much it would be hard to keep up with one more box.

"But Laura loves a tree. And loved these ornaments from the time she was a baby. And some painted egg-shells I had—that child was a fool for color. She wanted to know what hen laid the gloried eggs—that's what she called them—and when I explained they were painted that way, she was insulted. 'God should have done that Himself,' she announced. Did you ever hear of such a child?"

"She sounds like a combination of Anna and Helen."

"I wish she could see them then. It might soften her toward a child. Laura needs . . . but what am I doing, running on like this? *We* need to clear these boxes away before I start dinner. Tomorrow we'll see Laura. You can tell me if she's like your sisters then."

As we pack up the boxes, it's not Aunt Laura I'm thinking of. It's Mama and William. She must still love him to give Willie his name. And I wonder: When I threw the gravy boat, did it made her think of the star?

16

Today we're going to see Aunt Laura, to meet her for lunch at the Peabody Hotel. I wear my best dress—gray wool with a lace collar. At home it looks passable, but here—I don't know—I feel country. I think it's more my face than the dress.

"Your face is fine," Mama always says when she catches me frowning in the mirror. "Just don't go and wrinkle it up."

That's easy for her to say; Mama's face is doll-sweet. Mine is long and strong like a lantern, and I have dark hair thick enough to put out the light. I look in the mirror and think it's got to be a mask: I live here and I know I don't look like that.

But Omie looks exactly like herself, all rose, powdered and brushed, somewhere between flesh and china. I'll like being an old lady if I look like that.

"Let's go," she says, "or we'll be late for waiting."

"Pardon?"

"Laura never gets anywhere on time. Your grandfather says not a soul will come to her funeral."

"Her *funeral?*"

"Says they'll be afraid she won't show up."

Omie laughs, but I don't think it's funny. Just yesterday she told me about William who *did* die.

My coat feels thick against such mild weather. We walk two blocks to the Water Maple streetcar stop.

"You used to called these 'road trains,'" Omie says as we step up into the green and gold car. "Asked your daddy why they didn't haul coal."

I wish she wouldn't announce that I'm out of place. People are already staring.

We find a slatted bench and sit down just as the trolley lurches. Clack-clack-screech. David would love this, a train running through the middle of the road, dividing the traffic. But you'd have to blindfold Ben to get him on it. He'd see it as an insult to horses.

As we rattle along I look at street names, store names: Washington, Adams, Broadnax. We pass Court Square, the Orpheum Theater, words Mama says the way Daddy names trees.

We get off at Union. The Peabody's just around the corner. Omie walks as though someone had rolled out a carpet. I hurry beside her, hair flopping.

Then we arrive. A black man opens the door for us, and we step onto red carpet springy as moss. The walls are white marble. In the center of the lobby is the fountain, its famous ducks paddling.

"Those ducks live on the roof, you know."

"Mama told me."

"Every morning they come down on the elevator, walk across the carpet, and climb in. It gets the Peabody a lot of visitors."

"I guess so. I'd come here to see it."

"Really? I think it's disgraceful, making ducks go to work."

You never know what Omie is going to say.

"Let's find a seat. Only a statue could wait for Laura standing up."

So we sit. On a green velvet loveseat. I look at my fingernails. I am not going to gawk. I'll look around a little at a time. There's a gold chandelier like a lily above us, and sconces on the wall like . . .

"Good heavens, she's here!" Omie declares, lifting her shoulders, pulling back her chin.

Aunt Laura comes through the beveled doors like a movie star looking for a camera. I've never seen such clothes: a white flapper dress, a snug purple hat, a rope of pearls long enough to jump. The strange thing is she looks like Mama, except for being tall. Mama with money, no children, and enough sleep.

"Laura," Omie begins, standing up and looking stern, "you remember Mandy."

"Oh, yes," Aunt Laura cries, taking my hand in both of hers. "What a grown-up girl you're becoming!"

Putting her hands on my shoulders, she turns me around.

"You're going to be tall, that's a fact," she says, as though reading it in my backbone. "You'll have to stand straight, Mandy, and carry your height like it's the most valuable thing in the world."

I try to adjust.

"There," she says, "that's better. You need some other clothes, though. That color is . . ."

"Laura!" Omie hisses. "Let the child be!"

If you argue over me, I want to say, this is not going to be much fun. But I just follow them into the dining room.

The menu makes me wish for Mr. Aden. Shrimp creole? Coquille St. Jacques? Steak au poivre? There's fried chicken, too, but I don't want that. I didn't come here to eat something I could fix myself.

Aunt Laura sees me hesitate.

"Have you ever had scallops, Mandy?"

The only scallops I know you cut out of paper or cloth.

"What are they?"

"A kind of seafood. You should try them—the Co-quille. They're mild and delicious."

So that's what I order, saying "I'll have the Co-key-ya," trying not to feel like a fool. And when the food comes, it's wonderful, little rubbery nubs in a white sauce, served in a real scallop shell! It's hard to believe. Me, Mandy Perritt, eating such food in a dining room bigger than my house. And Aunt Laura complaining because there are no grown-up drinks. And Omie suggesting baked Alaska for dessert.

Now that is something to tell the boys about. It's better than ducks in the lobby. Ice cream *on fire*. It's inside a dome made of egg whites and sugar, and they put some special drink on it and set it ablaze.

When the waiter brings it to our table, it looks big as a volcano. I'm glad to find it's for all of us. Omie and I eat most of it, though. Aunt Laura says she has to think of her clothes.

"What do you mean?" We all have great big napkins, and I wouldn't think she'd be messy anyway.

"She means," Omie answers, "that she's afraid she might take on flesh. As if she weren't too skinny to begin with. What a man wants with a woman who looks like a coat hanger, I don't know."

"Yes," Aunt Laura flashes, "and you don't know what I want with Cress either."

"Let's not get into that."

Aunt Laura looks hard at Omie. Then she takes from her purse a gold box and takes from the box a cigarette, and, looking like she owns the world, lights it in the Peabody Hotel. Omie's eyes blaze. But she doesn't speak. She reckons the bill and signals our waiter.

On the way out I ask Omie if the duck pond is for wishes.

"If you can wish without throwing money," she says. "What comes off the coins can poison the ducks. Trouble is, most people think wishing *is* throwing money, throwing it by the handfuls into wild and useless places. But you can wish by just touching the water. It's the water that God made, not the coins."

I go over to do that, and while my back is to them Aunt Laura slips away.

*   *   *

Coming home on the streetcar I ask Omie about Uncle Cress. What had Aunt Laura meant about her not liking him?

"That's just grown-up talk, Mandy. Don't bother your head about it."

"Does that mean I won't get to go and see them?"

"No, not at all. And Mandy, try not to listen so hard."

I've thought about that and I must say, for once, I think Omie is wrong. If I don't listen hard and bother my head, how am I ever going to know anything? She thinks I'm a child when I've already been a mother. I'm overdue for learning. I've got to watch and listen and read and ask and bother. That's how the great scientists work. Mr. Aden told us at school.

"They take nothing for granted. No mere notion of the earth contents them. Nor of the sea, the sky, the landscape of their own street. They mean to see it in a new way, to find its secrets."

That's me exactly. And I can't do that without bothering my head.

17

Christmas Eve. In Goose Rock Mama will put holly on the mantel. Daddy will set up the tree. Before bed, they'll pop corn on the fire and light the candles. With Mama playing the piano, everyone will sing:

> *O little town of Bethlehem*
> *How still we see thee lie.*

Mama has a hymnal, so they don't miss a verse. Anna and Helen hum when they run out of words.

> *O morning stars together*
> *Proclaim His holy birth.*

After that, Daddy always says, "I used to know some of those Morningstars. Had a farm over in Knott County. Couldn't get to the end of a furrow but they'd proclaim."

"Jim," Mama says, and that stops him. It's a dance they do.

But here it's different. The tree has been up two

days. The house is still. Omie gives me a rope of pine to wind down the stair rail. We chop onions and celery.

After supper things move faster. We have to clean up the kitchen and get ready for church. It doesn't start till eleven o'clock. I've never gone to a service that late. Omie explains, "We always have midnight service come Christmas and Easter. Most babies come at night, you know."

"But what's Easter got to do with babies?"

"Christmas is Jesus' birthday, but Easter is ours. Light out of darkness, life everlasting. Who wouldn't wait up for that?"

A lot of people. I try to imagine getting us all to Manchester over muddy spring roads at night. But this is Memphis: brick streets, motor cars. And only the three of us.

When I start upstairs to change, Omie calls, "Look in your closet for a present."

I know better than to bound up the stairs like I'm doing. But I can't wait! I slow down just a little bit opening the closet door.

There's a new dress hanging between my old ones— low waisted, Christmas green. It's velvet and smells elegant. It even looks good when I put it on! In a dress this shape, it's okay to be skinny, and the color makes me look softer. I pull my hair back. When it gets longer . . . but I have to go show Omie.

"That's just right," she says, after I turn around for her in the middle of the hall. "Laura said that style would suit you."

"Aunt Laura picked it?"

"No, but she told me what to get."

"Does she choose your clothes?"

"Heavens, no. She thinks I dress like a footstool."

"Well, I don't. And I love this, whoever picked it. Thank you so much." I give Omie a hug.

"Then go change your shoes and we'll be off. Opie's warming up the car."

Church at home is wooden and Presbyterian; the windows are swirls of yellow and green, cheaper than stained glass. Omie and Opie go to the Episcopal Church. It's gray stone with color leaded in the windows. Red, yellow, and blue stream out into the dark. People are hushed as they move along the walk and up the steps.

The small church wavers in candlelight. We squeeze into a middle pew, but the people after us have to stand in the back. Everyone is singing "Hark, the Herald" and then "We Three Kings." Where we have a communion table, the Episcopals have an altar, all gold, with a wooden crucifix hanging above it. Poor naked Jesus! He makes me nervous, nailed up there like a hide to somebody's barn.

But in front of the altar there's a manger scene. "Crèche," Omie calls it. Wise men and beasts, shepherds and camels, and the family. One angel. It makes me think of Anna and Helen. I wonder if their ornaments are on our tree.

The best things about the church are the music and the windows. And they fit together. Organ music is rich and excited, like darkness broken into light. Each windowsill has pine boughs and candles. We keep singing: "The First Noel," "Angels We Have Heard on High." Opie explains that we sing right up to midnight, when Jesus is born. Then he yawns. I don't suppose anybody sang for Mary birthing Jesus. Nobody sang for Mama and Willie.

Then the organ begins "Brightest and Best":

> *Brightest and best*
> *Of the sons of the morning*

It's a mountain tune, steep and mournful. How did they get it here?

> *Dawn on our darkness*
> *And lend us thine aid.*

I can hear Daddy's voice, feel it tremble the hymnal as we go into the low part:

> *Star of the East*
> *The horizon adorning*

Last year Helen couldn't say "horizon adorning," and Ben's voice turned high when he tried to send it low.

> *Guide where our Infant*
> *Redeemer is laid.*

Mama used to look at Helen as she sang that. This year it will be Willie. I'm not there to see it and I'm crying. Omie bends down.

"If we were good enough for our babies," she whispers, "we could do our own redeeming."

She reaches behind me to Opie to prod him awake.

18

When I wake up, daylight is standing in my room. I've never slept till light on Christmas and my heart lurches, afraid I've missed the whole day. At home Helen will be back to sleep now, exhausted by candy canes and a doll. Mama will have the turkey baking. And what about Willie?

I find Omie and Opie in the kitchen. He's dusting two picnic hampers and she's working a golden turkey leg like a pump handle.

"I don't want to rush it, but I think it's done. What do you think?"

"Just tell me when to eat," Opie replies.

"Christmas gift," I tell them. The first one to make this greeting is supposed to have luck the whole year.

"Oh, Mandy, you're up. Now we'll have to have presents, and there's so much to do. . . ."

"Easy, Miss Anna," Opie tells her. "None of us will starve."

"But Laura and Cress will be there at two o'clock."

"Be where?"

"This year I really didn't think it would be fair."

"What would be fair?"

"The weather. So I hadn't prepared—"

"Opie, what is she talking about?"

"Surely Rena's told you. Christmas dinner outside: it's an all-fired Ezelle tradition. Doesn't have to be warm, mind you, just sunlight somewhere south of a snowbank."

"You know you love every minute of it."

"Yes, indeed. Broccoli's hearty. A little frost never hurt it. And snowflake potatoes . . ."

He holds his big hands palms up, as if to ask "Why me?"

"You mean we're going to eat Christmas dinner *outside?*"

"Yes," Omie says, leaning with her rolling pin into the roll dough. "In the shelterhouse at Overton Park. Weather permitting, we always do. And your grandfather always behaves like this."

"What can I do?" I ask.

"Help yourself to some ham and beaten biscuit. Opie, pour the child some coffee."

Perched on a kitchen stool, I eat, watching Omie do four things while Opie does one.

"I can take the gravy in one jar, the cranberry sauce in another. The oyster dressing can go in its baking dish . . . Mandy, come peel potatoes . . . the rolls in their pan wrapped in towels. You will build a fire, won't you?"

"Me?"

"No, no, child. Mr. Culton, you will build a fire at the park?"

Opie looks up from polishing each strand of the honeysuckle basket.

"A fire? Only four days past the winter solstice?"

"To keep the food warm."

"Yes, ma'am."

Have they forgotten it's Christmas?

But once I've got the potatoes boiling, Omie says it's time to go look at the tree. I have two presents; I open the one from Omie and Opie first. It's in a silver box, tied with blue ribbon. There's cotton inside, and inside the cotton, a gold locket big as a half dollar! It has flowers engraved on one side and my initials on the back:

A.V.P.

When I open it, Omie and Opie look back at me, tiny faces snipped from a photograph.

"We want you to keep us close to your heart," Omie says, slipping the long chain over my head.

"It's beautiful. Thank you. Thank you, Opie." I kiss his cool rough cheek.

"Now see what Rena sent."

He hands me a flat, rounded package, something soft, not in a box. Forgetting to save the paper, I tear into it, through several layers of tissue.

It's a shawl of flowers and leaves, crocheted in white baby yarn. Holding it close, I smell home.

"When did Mama do this?"

"While she was in bed, she told me. Used to hide it under the covers when you came in."

"But I changed the bed."

"Rena's quicker than that."

"Stand up," Omie says, "and try it on."

I feel a little stiff and silly, but the shawl is so elegant that once it's on, I start to feel elegant, too.

"Pretty as a picture," Opie judges.

He doesn't say of what.

Omie has given Opie a tie and a new pipe. Daddy sent him a pipestand, carved from a single piece of cherry.

"Now that's masterful." Opie turns it over in his hands, tracing the woodgrain. "A man who could do that ought to be carving newel posts and moldings."

Opie has for Omie an opal pendant. It's her birthstone.

"Now don't take on," he says, before she even gets started.

"But I love it."

"I just went into Ostriker's and said, 'What goes well with a woman with freckledy eyes?' "

Omie's eyes are opalescent.

Of course I know what Mama sent her: two dogwood and two redbud starts.

"Just what we're needing!" Omie exclaims. "Trust Rena to send spring. I had told her about losing that magnolia—"

"You can't expect these little fellows to replace that."

"You can't replace a tree anyway. Like people, you don't know how big they were till they're gone. But it's good to have new trees."

"Why don't you plant them today, since it's picnic weather?"

The look she gives him is almost shy.

It takes a long time to get Christmas dinner on the road. When we're finally loaded into the car, windows fogged by the steam, the sky rumbles.

"That's the blessing," Opie says.

Aunt Laura and Uncle Cress are late. We've put down the cloth, set the table—with a centerpiece of pine cones and branches—placed the food, and covered it all with blankets. Then we wait. A wind is starting by the time we hear them get out of their car.

Uncle Cress's voice booms in the cold air:

Good King Wenceslas looked out

Aunt Laura answers out of tune:

On the feast of Stephen

Uncle Cress picks it up again:

When the snow lay round about

"Round about!" Aunt Laura shouts.

And dinner was uneaten!

A duet of laughter. Both appear in matching raccoon coats.

"Merry Christmas!"

"Christmas gift!"

"Joyeux Noel, Anna Ezelle!"

Aunt Laura hugs Omie, who stands still as a park statue.

"Amanda!" Aunt Laura breaks the silence. "You remember your Uncle Cress? Cresswell, this is Amanda Virginia Perritt."

"So it is," he says, offering me his hand. I'd forgotten how handsome he is, blond, smooth-faced, except for a mustache that curls.

Omie stares at us all till we sit down.

"Grace, please."

"Our Father," Opie begins, but in his Southern speech it sounds like Owl Feather.

"Bless the hands that prepared it," Opie is saying. A crow calls like a rusty hinge.

"Bless it to our use and us to Thy service. Amen."

"Amen."

Omie rolls the blankets off the food.

"Voilà!" Aunt Laura claps her hands. "Better than the magician yanking the cloth from beneath the dishes."

"I just hope it's warmer than this stone bench." Omie shivers. Is she scolding Aunt Laura for being late?

"Everybody up!" Opie orders. We stand while he spreads blankets on the benches. "Coffee?" he looks at Omie.

"Let's save that," she says. "We may need it to thaw out at the end of the meal."

We all sit down.

"Oyster dressing!" Cress exclaims. "Why didn't you teach your daughter to make this?"

"Never could get her in the kitchen."

"Now, Mother."

"Or I never could get her to stand still. She danced, posed in doorways, draped tablecloths around her."

Cress takes a bottle from inside his coat and pours something in his cup.

"Mr. Culton?"

"Thank you."

Aunt Laura holds up hers.

"But Rena played the piano."

"Only in the parlor. She didn't practice any scales on the kitchen counter."

"She did in church. On her lap. And she had that paper keyboard—"

"She had what?"

"A paper keyboard she pasted on an old box. Used to practice up in our room when you said it was too late to play."

Mama?

"I can still see her sitting up in bed in that raggedy nightgown—"

"My child never—"

"You threw it away but she found it. Practicing Chopin. Biting her lip, tossing her head, till I almost heard the music too."

"I never knew that."

"That was when you had the bad leg. You never came upstairs." A laugh simmers. "We still had the outhouse way at the back of the yard. And you had that cane-bottomed chair, remember? We could see you with your leg bent, resting your knee in that old chair, making for the outhouse."

She looks at Uncle Cress.

"Mother said she had to start out long before she wanted to go."

Aunt Laura's laugh bubbles over. Cress and I join her; even Opie chuckles. But Omie looks at Aunt Laura's untouched plate.

"The spirit of Christmas doesn't come in a bottle."

We don't say much after that. I like the cold food, though. All the tastes are clearer out here.

"Now for the crown," Opie says. "Where's the plum pudding?"

Omie uncovers it.

"Bravo! Another rabbit!" Aunt Laura sings.

"Let me get the hard sauce from the fire." Omie gets up with some trouble. "This cold will make an old woman of me. Opie, you do the honors."

He takes a bottle from the hamper and drizzles its contents over the dark, fluted cake. It smells like sweet wood. *Scratch*—the flame leaps, covering the little dome. Opie jumps back.

"God bless us! Now where's the coffee?"

Omie produces that, too, pouring it from a thermos jug while the halo of fire flashes out.

"Laura, would you serve the pudding?"

"That I can do," Aunt Laura says, rising. "I'm an expert slicer."

When Opie takes his first bite, he sighs. "Topsoil couldn't taste sweeter to a maple."

Everybody laughs this time, settling down to the last taste of Christmas. Opie lights candles. We're alone in the park, the winter day fading. Just ahead of night, we pack up and drive home.

19

The next morning Omie is tired.

"I'm not going to do a thing today but wash and put away dishes. That's no fun. Why don't you go with Opie to the mill?"

Sawdust piles, bandsaws, men with fingers gone: that doesn't sound like much fun either. But I don't want to hurt her feelings.

"I'd love to."

"All right," Opie says. "But first we'll have to get these Christmas trees in the ground."

For a minute I think he means the tree we decorated. But then he goes on: "Rena's mountain sprouts. They've been out of earth long enough."

So out we go after breakfast with a spade and a post-hole digger. We start in the side yard next to the corner. The ground is soft, and Opie's used to this. He takes a neat tube of dirt out with the digger and leaves me to spade dirt loose around it. On he goes to the front.

Omie wants one dogwood in front of the house,

one in back, and the redbuds on either side. "That way," she says, "I'll see spring out every window."

"And see Rena," Opie adds.

He plants trees the way Mama makes biscuits, as if it's as natural as breathing. His big hands pat the reddish dirt into place.

"That ought to hold," he says, as we finish the last of the redbuds. "Let's get them a drink."

He carries that to them in a tin watering can. Then we wash up and set off for the mill.

Memphis is bustling this day after Christmas. I'm surprised, but Opie explains, "Folks have to change what's the wrong color or what they got two of or what's too big in the seat."

"But why today?"

"Something to do. Can't just sit looking at a turkey carcass and a dead tree."

"Opie, tell me something about Mama."

"Well, she was the first person to call me Opie. She couldn't call me Papa, so soon after losing her own. And I called her Dumpling—till she got big enough to ask me to stop."

"I mean about her music and Aunt Laura and—"

"Whoa, there. One thing at a time."

"How much older is Mama than Aunt Laura?"

"Hmm. Let me see. Some of those years were longer than others." He studies the road.

"How old was Mama when you married Omie?"

"Who are you—some reporter from *The Commercial Appeal*?"

"I think she said she was three."

"Sounds right."

"So when was Aunt Laura born?"

"Well, there's William, Lizzie, Anna May—I guess about thirteen years."

"What?"

"Separating Rena and Laura. Laura's the baby, as if you couldn't tell."

"That's almost the same as me and Willie. I turned twelve just before he was born."

"Step careful then. Your mama hung over Laura like a guardian angel. And Laura broke every string in her harp."

"What do you mean?"

"Cried herself sick whenever Jim Perritt came courting. Didn't want Rena out of her sight."

"She didn't like Daddy?"

"Only time he took her on his lap she bit him on the cheek."

Seems like I shouldn't laugh at that but I do.

"What about the music?"

"That's different."

We're out of town now, turned onto a red clay road.
"How?"

"You get Omie to tell you about that."

"Will she?"

"Don't ask me. We've only been married thirty years."

The road takes us out of trees and into big flatlands along the river.

"Just a couple more miles," Opie says.

We ride in silence.

"Cotton, timber, pallets—all kinds of businesses latch

onto the Mississippi. Like fleas on a dog. Here's my flea."

We drive through a gate into a graveled yard. The road goes between big stacks of lumber. I don't see any sawdust, worksheds, or sawyers. Just a one-room building painted white.

"That can't be the chowhouse."

"Not hardly. I figured you'd seen plenty of sawmills, so I brought you down to the shipping yard. All we do here is fill the orders. Operate out of that office."

Opie pulls up next to it.

"Well, come on in."

The little room is full of dust and old pipe smoke. Penciled notes on different colored paper are taped on the desk, the filing cabinet, the wall.

"What are these?"

"My employees."

"They write you notes? But they all look like the same hand."

"Now you're a detective. They are. They're my notes."

"But why?"

Opie rubs his forehead.

"Times aren't hard just in Goose Rock. I've had to let my bookkeeper go and do it myself. The notes remind me what to do when."

"Will that work?"

"I hope so. Business is slower, which gives me more time and fewer accounts."

He shifts a ledger on the desk, reads one note. "We're not working today."

"I guess nobody returns Christmas boards."

"That's right." He smiles. "Let's go pay tribute to the river."

Walking between stacks of sweet-smelling lumber, I think of Daddy. I forget how it was that he took just me up on Big Lick, but he did once, and we were walking like this.

"Mandy," he said, "you're breathing the smell of promise. This timber's going to be houses, good houses for miners, put up by the Darby Coal. I've sold so much to the mines—roof beams and timbers—I'm glad to sell them something that won't go underground."

"Are these houses, Opie?"

"What, child?"

"Are these lumber piles going to be houses?"

"I hope so."

"Don't you know?"

"And don't you know when to stop asking questions? I swear, you're as bad as Laura used to be."

Opie smiles, but I can tell he's not entirely kidding. We walk on to the river without a word.

If you've never seen the Mississippi, you probably think like I did that a river is just a minor exception to land. Sometimes flooding, other times drying up, but still an exception. Not the Mississippi. It's a fact. I can hardly see across it.

"Is this the widest part?"

"Not quite. It's wider at the Delta."

"Is the ocean like this?"

"I don't think so. From what I hear, the ocean is blue and comes right at you."

"You've never seen it?"

"Nope."

"But Opie, you ought to. You're getting old."

I wish I could take that back as soon as I say it. What's got into me?

But Opie chuckles.

"Old and hungry, that's me. Let's go home and see if there's any meat left on that bird."

20

We drowsed away the rest of yesterday. I read Keats' "Nightingale" which is sleepy too. But today Aunt Laura has volunteered to take me sightseeing. I can't wait!

"It's a sight what you'll see with Laura, that's for sure," Opie says over breakfast. "But you might like to look at this first."

He hands me a letter from the stack of mail Omie brought in. It's from Mama.

"And here's yours." He slides another one across the table to Omie.

I've never had a letter from Mama before. *Miss Amanda Perritt:* her handwriting, plain as day. Opie has already slit the envelope with his pen knife; I fish out the single sheet.

Sunday, December 21
Goose Rock

Dear Amanda,
Merry Christmas to my first daughter! I hope you are enjoying your holiday and remembering your manners.

Your father put the tree up today—a handsome fir—so the house smells like the woods and he felt right at home.

Willie is trying very hard to roll over. Anna and Helen coax him, not knowing the work when he begins to crawl. You remember keeping up with Helen.

With school out this week, David and Ben have gone to help at the mill and the house is awfully quiet.

Kiss Omie and Opie for me and come home soon. We miss you.

Love,
Mama
Mrs. James D. Perritt

When I finish the letter, it's a shock to be in Memphis. I feel like I've stood in the door at home.

Opie is drawing a map to the streetcar stop.

"Put in Johnson School," Omie reminds him.

He does. Neatly. They debate about how much money I need. Finally, mid-morning, they let me set off.

I try to look like I've waited for streetcars all my life.

"Where are you visiting from, honey?" says a lady in a cranberry coat.

"Kentucky."

"Daniel Boone's country."

"Yes, ma'am."

She probably thinks we wear coonskin caps and eat deer meat.

"Don't worry about getting lost. The conductor will help you. We're all friendly down here."

"Thank you." I dread more help.

But when the streetcar comes we get separated, so I don't have to worry. I get off at Second and make my transfer for Catalpa with no problem.

I could pick out Aunt Laura's door even if I didn't know the number. All the other houses have lace panels behind the side glass. Aunt Laura's curtains are two shades of purple.

When she lets me in, I see there are curtains in the other doorways, too, tied or pushed to one side— yellow, orange, white.

"Your house doesn't look like this," Aunt Laura laughs.

"Not exactly."

"You probably have furniture. Tables, chairs. If you do that, you have to decide which room is which."

"Don't you?"

"Sometimes this is the living room," she says, as we walk into the room off the hall. It has bare floors, a rag rug, and one big straw chair.

"And we eat here sometimes." She gestures to the next room, with a wooden card table in the center and big pink and gold pillows piled under the window. "We can sit on the floor, we can sit at the table. Or we can switch the two rooms around." She makes it sound like great fun.

"But I do know where the bedroom is. Come back with me while I finish my face."

I follow her down a narrow hall and through a doorway hung with beads. Really. They rattle as I walk through. She laughs.

"Mother says I'm a genius at furnishing doorways."

Curtains are shut in the bedroom, so it's dim despite the bright day. Aunt Laura waves toward a cloud of clothes heaped on the unmade bed.

"I've been going through things this morning, clearing out for the new year, and I wonder if there's anything there you could use."

I look at her. There's a difference between having your clothes on and being dressed. She's dressed: black chemise, red shoes, red beads, and fingernails red as fire. And her cast-off clothes will be for getting dressed, too. In Goose Rock you put your clothes on.

She sits down at her dressing table.

"Oh, Amanda, I forgot to take your coat. Just hang it on the bedpost."

I do, and she gets to work, licking an eyebrow pencil, leaning intently toward herself. I sort out the delicate dresses, feeling like a chowhouse dish beside china. These aren't for me—a yellow crepe scoop-necked shimmy, a lavender square-cut shift.

"At least try the red one."

I untangle it and find buttons smaller than baby teeth, a straight skirt, a flounce to let you walk. Can you see me headed up the dirt road to school in this?

But she's saying to try it on—

"No, you ninny, you have to take your clothes off first!"

I feel more naked standing here in my slip than bathing in the kitchen at home. I try to hurry, but the dress sticks at my shoulders, my hipbones. Finally I get it on, pull it straight.

Aunt Laura watches from the mirror.

"Not bad," she says. "Come let me see."

She tilts her head and studies me. Her red mouth curls.

"I used to look just like you."

"You did not." That pops out before I can stop it.

"I did too. I was tall and skinny, what they call a carpenter's dream."

"Pardon?"

"Flat as a board. And I slumped to apologize for taking up space."

"Your face never looked like mine."

"No, yours is stronger. And your eyes are like amber. The dress isn't right but the color is. Amanda—"

I hate being inspected by someone so pretty.

"What?"

"Did you ever have a doll?"

"I had Beverly."

"And clothes for her."

"All that Mama had time to make."

"No matter what you put on her she looked the same, right?"

I nod. I didn't come over here to talk about dolls.

"But people aren't like that. They change. The doll is all on the outside."

I wait for her to get to the point.

"So the outside has to be perfect. But what people have on the inside changes how they look. Of course, hairstyle helps and makeup—"

"What you're saying is I'm not pretty but I'm nice."

She laughs.

"You're stubborn, I'll say that. Like Mother and me and Rena."

"Is that bad?"

"I'd say it's good, the world being what it is. But that's another story. I'm ready. You get your clothes on and let's see what we can see."

21

I feel so lucky to be going out with Aunt Laura. I don't know where—maybe a play or a concert. You can't even go to a picture show in Goose Rock. Besides, I want to see something on a stage. I want to sit in the dark and see something—

"Amanda!"

"What?"

"This is the streetcar stop."

"Sorry."

"You were a million miles away. Homesick, I'll bet."

I don't say anything.

"You can't tell me you don't miss Duck Roost."

The Number Eight car rattles up and we get in. We have to sit in front, right behind the driver.

"It's Goose Rock. And no, I don't. I miss Willie sometimes and maybe Helen."

"And your little place by the hearth?"

"You missed Mama pretty bad when she started courting Daddy."

"Trust Mother to bring that up."

"It's all right to miss people."

"Not for me, Amanda. I've got to *have* them."

"But Mama's still your sister."

"She's no more mine than a toy that's rolled out of reach. Cress is my sister now."

"Uncle Cress?"

"And brother and father and mother, and babies and Holy Confessor."

"But Omie and Opie are right here in town."

"They are not right here. They're all the way over on Poplar."

"But Aunt Laura—"

"Amanda, this is a silly topic for discussion. Let's put it away. And pay attention now. The next stop is ours."

We get off on Main Street, but not at a place I've seen before. Aunt Laura herds me across the pavement.

"Do you like sweet potatoes?"

"Pardon?"

"Yams, I mean. And trumpet music and straw hats?"

"Well, sure—"

"Good. That settles it. We're going down Beale Street."

She looks at me, waiting.

"You don't know what that is?"

"No."

"We'll fix that."

Most of the people on the busy street are black. Small stores are jumbled together. One building says Manhattan Saloon right on it. Aunt Laura seems completely at home, but I feel funny.

"What do people do here?"

"Why, they buy shirts, Amanda. Shirts and beans and liquor, when they can get it. They go to the bank. See that building over there? That's the first negro bank in Memphis. And more than that, on Saturday night, they make the best music in the world."

"What kind of music?"

"Oh, not like anything you've ever heard. It's wild and loud. Not a bit like white music."

I didn't know music came in colors.

"Come on, let's see what's in here," Aunt Laura says, steering me into the nearest shop. Parrot-colored shirts, straw hats, and shoes spill over in the tiny space.

Aunt Laura slips out of her hard red shoes and into a pair of soft straw ones. She tries hats till she finds one that fits, then plops it on and poses, waiting for someone to admire her. We could be pieces of lint on the floor for all the black people notice. They're talking and laughing and figuring their own purchases.

"How do I look?" Aunt Laura asks.

"Wonderful."

"You try some, too, Amanda."

"I wouldn't have anywhere to wear something like that."

"That's not the point. Just try them for the fun of it."

I do, but it hurts to see my face hard and worried underneath that happy hat. Aunt Laura looks like she's never worn anything else.

I put the hat back in the big cardboard box.

"Could we go now?"

"Oh, Mandy. You are a case."

A case? What's that supposed to mean? A case of measles? A case of canned goods?

"Let me at least get you a pair of straw shoes." She rummages through another box. "Here. Try these."

They're like walking on a hay bale.

"Do they fit?"

"Yes, but—"

"What?"

"There's nowhere I can wear them."

"Let them be bedroom slippers. Wear them to the beach."

"We don't have a beach."

"You used to. Used to be all ocean up there. That's how you got the sandstone."

"Mr. Aden told us about that."

"So you see, you can wear them to the beach. You'll just be a little late."

I have to laugh at that.

Back on the street Aunt Laura strolls like the queen of the King Cotton parade. Never mind that the straw hat is silly in winter or that people look right through us. I try to stand up straight.

We've been walking for a couple of blocks when Aunt Laura points to a small sign across the street. SULTANNA'S it says, the name circled with a string of Christmas lights.

"Next stop," Aunt Laura declares.

At first it seems cave-dark in the little restaurant, but as my eyes adjust, I see a bunch of tables, mostly for two or three people, and some stools around a long bar to the back. I know it's a bar because I saw one at the Peabody. There's no one buying drinks. Right now there's a law against it.

Daddy says you might as well make a law against having babies as against buying liquor. I don't see what babies have to do with it.

The unfinished floor makes me think of the Manchester Hardware. There are chipped black tables with fruit jar lids for ashtrays, and a loud sour smell on top of everything. Underneath is a good smell though, like cinnamon toast.

A coffee-colored woman comes over to our table.

"I'll have a fizz," Aunt Laura tells her. "And a plate of logs, please. Mandy, what would you like—a cherry Coke? a sarsaparilla?"

"A sarsaparilla."

I'm not sure what that is, but it sounds good.

In a minute the kitchen door swings open and the waitress comes out with a tray balanced on her shoulder. That sweet smell comes with her. It's yam slices, deep fried and rolled in cinnamon sugar! They're good as doughnuts. And the sarsaparilla tickles my nose.

Aunt Laura only nibbles at one log, but she drinks her fizz straight down.

"I'll have another," she calls to the waitress.

"I like it here."

"Good for you. Your grandmother probably won't like it that I brought you."

"Has she been here?"

"No. I've tried to bring her. She seems to sing best in her own cage."

"What?"

"She has her own Memphis, that's all. Are you finished?"

"One more log."

"Okay. Then let's get going."

When she stands, Aunt Laura wobbles a little.

"I should have bought straw shoes, too," she says. "A day in these heels can cripple you."

There's no one in sight to pay, so Aunt Laura leaves a few curling bills and a mound of change on the table. I'm shocked. Where I come from you count. Even the pennies.

For a minute, as we come out of Sultanna's and into the sunlight, none of this seems real: Beale Street, sarsaparilla, Aunt Laura. It's like something I made up. The real thing is Goose Rock, Daddy figuring in the ledger, Mama saying, "Use it up, wear it out, make it do."

Aunt Laura breaks the spell.

"One more thing we need to do for you, Amanda. We need to find you some music."

"But I can't stay till tonight."

"It's a shame, too. But somebody will be playing to fill a hat down in Crawfish Alley."

Before we go another block, Aunt Laura guides me into a gap between buildings and, sure enough, there sits a man playing a long black horn. It sounds like a bird squealing.

I know birds don't squeal, but if they did they would sound like this. Squealing in tune, mind you. Squealing with joy and pain and fear—maybe about how birds have to fly but this one doesn't want to. How does it know its wings will work? Or what to do when the wind changes? Or how to slow down and hook a branch with its claws?

Aunt Laura says Omie keeps to her cage. Does that mean she'll never hear this music? Mama sure doesn't hear it in Goose Rock. And how can she get out? She's surrounded: mountains, children. She'd have to fly. But the music says that's so hard . . .

I look at Aunt Laura, her eyes closed, leaning against the dirty wall.

Suddenly the musician stops and looks up at me, his dark eyes squinting.

"Humph," he says to Aunt Laura. "Looks like your rose done caught her heart on a thorn."

Aunt Laura stands straight.

"Why, Amanda, whatever is the matter?"

Tears roll down my neck. "It's just the music. It's so . . ." I can't explain. "It's so big."

"Yes, indeed, it is that." Aunt Laura laughs. She opens her purse, takes out another curl of bills, and tosses them in the player's hat. "You're Rena's daughter all right," she says, resting her hand on my shoulder. "Come on, Amanda. It's time we were getting you home."

Light is wearing out as we walk to the top of Beale Street.

"Aunt Laura, what happened to Mama's music?"

"I guess it's in the attic somewhere if she didn't take it with her."

"I mean her playing. It must have meant a lot to her—"

"Everything."

"Now she only plays 'Rock of Ages' or 'Turkey in the Straw.'"

"Jim Perritt happened to it."

"But Daddy likes her to play."

"Sure he does—in a cabin a hundred miles from nowhere."

"We've never lived in a cabin."

"You know what I mean."

"Well, why did she go?"

"Your Daddy, like I said."

"Why didn't they stay here?"

"Jim Perritt said he had no mind to work timber in land so flat you could mow it down. Mountains are like rivers: they get in your blood."

"But not in Mama's?"

"No, hers was pure music."

"Then I don't understand—"

"That makes two of us."

"I mean how she can stand not to play now."

"Probably better than she could stand the sound if she did."

"But that's terrible!"

"Yes, but look at it this way: Where would you be if music was the center of her life?"

There's nothing to say to that.

"This is my stop. Can you go the rest of the way yourself?"

"Sure. I've got Opie's map."

She goes down the aisle and calls back from the door.

"I've had hundreds. They don't help. But they give you something to look at when you're lost."

We both laugh as she swings down onto the street. I watch out the window but in half a minute she's gone.

22

 I'm just going to ask Omie is all. I want to know and people don't volunteer telling. There's only today and tomorrow before I go home, and tomorrow I'm going back to Aunt Laura's.

Today is Sunday—still as a dead rabbit. We went to church but it wasn't like Christmas, ate dinner, and now we're sunk into the parlor, Opie asleep with the newspaper in his lap, Omie crocheting. Another popcorn-stitch bedspread. Every time she hooks the thread, I feel caught and twisted. If I'm going to ask, I have to ask now.

"Omie?"

"Yes, child."

Our words hang between ticks of the grandfather clock.

"Why did Mama give up music for Daddy?"

"Who said she did?"

"Aunt Laura. She said music meant everything to Mama until Daddy took her away."

"That sounds like Laura."

"You mean it's not true?"

"I mean Laura only paints with shocking colors."

"But what about Mama staying up late practicing on cardboard?"

"I guess that's true. Probably it happened once or twice and Laura's made it a history. Laura didn't want to *lose* Rena, you see. They had their own world. And in crashed Jim Perritt."

"Did Mama want to go on the stage?"

"Rena? Heavens, no. Oh, she might have liked to play in an orchestra—I don't doubt that—but not by herself. And what kind of life is that? That's what I said to her—"

"So you talked her out of it?"

"No, ma'am, I did not." Omie snaps this out and bites off her thread. Opie stirs under the paper.

I'd better try another approach.

"Why didn't Aunt Laura want Mama to go?"

"Why is the grass green, Mandy? Why is red flannel?"

"I don't know."

And I don't know what's making her mad.

Omie looks at the circle she's finished, flattens it out on her skirt.

"I've always felt bad about Rena and Laura. It was my fault in a way. Laura was so little when William died and for a while—I don't know, I just couldn't stand a little child in my lap. Couldn't tie her jingle shoes without hearing William say 'I've got bells on so Mama won't get lost.'

"I guess it takes different women differently. I might have doted on Laura, never let her out of my sight. But instead I pulled back. And Rena was so eager. Like you, Mandy, she was a little mother from the start. . . . "

I remember my heart falling when Daddy put Willie in my arms.

"Laura latched on twice as hard, feeling I had left her. When other children called for Mama, she called 'Vrena!' And she loved your mother's music. Until she got too big, she'd sit in Rena's lap, still as a stone, while Rena practiced. 'Vrena has songs in her hands,' she told me.

"Rena dressed Laura in the morning, put her to bed at night. When your mama was at school I felt like I was just keeping Laura. And I know that's what Laura felt. It made me sad, but I couldn't change it. It was too late."

The loss in Omie's voice stirs something in me, too. Mama and Laura . . . I know that hurt. Where does it connect? Mama lifts Willie from my arms to bathe him for the first time. I stand at the kitchen sink in tears.

No wonder Mama sent me to Memphis. She was afraid of losing Willie to me. Are there always two stories going on like that?

"I don't know what Laura expected—your mother to go on the road and take her along like a suitcase?—but she didn't expect your mother to marry. And when Rena and Jim ran off—"

"Ran off?"

"Don't tell me you don't know that story."

"I don't."

"Heavenly days, child! Well, don't tell Rena I told you."

"So you didn't want her to marry Daddy either."

"Not at seventeen, I didn't. Opie told Jim just to wait a year or two, but no, Jim had to go back to the mountains and take a wife with him."

"How did they get away?"

"Rena said she was staying overnight at Corrie Landrum's and they left on the train."

Omie pulls up more thread.

"And you didn't know?"

"Of course I knew!"

The thread sticks. Omie leans on the arm of the wing-backed chair and tries to pull it free. When that doesn't work, she opens her sewing stand, where the big cone of thread has slipped from its spindle. She resets it.

"There!"

The crochet hook begins to tug at the line.

"How?"

"How what?"

I don't know if she's forgotten or just doesn't want to tell.

"How did you know?"

"Rena'd been acting over-ordinary, the way people do when they're about to upset everything. And after she left, Laura noticed something missing, I forget what, a thing she wouldn't have taken to Corrie's. So Opie went after them. Said he arrived at the same time as the train."

"Did they hide?"

"Your mama and daddy? Not for a minute. Jim Perritt just said he'd be proud to have Opie stand up with them. 'No sir,' said Opie, and that was that."

"What about Aunt Laura?"

"She cried like an orphan for longer than I care to remember. I could have skinned Rena. But there's nothing as hard as a young heart, Laura's included. You remember that."

What I remember is Aunt Laura on the streetcar, saying Mama is no more her sister now "than a toy that's rolled out of reach."

23

It's raining and the streetcar is crowded. I feel funny going to Aunt Laura's for lunch. Yesterday while Omie talked I felt I was meeting Aunt Laura as a little girl. But today at her house she'll be grown up.

Nobody pays me any mind. Does that mean I look like a city girl? Omie helped me pin my hair under.

I can tell as soon as I arrive that something is wrong. Old newspapers are piled on the porch and the curtains are drawn. Aunt Laura is slow in coming.

She has on a black satin bathrobe, shiny as coal and trailing all the way to the floor. It's tied with a gold cord, but looks like it might fall open or off anyway. Maybe I'm early and she's just gotten out of the bath. But she doesn't have that kind of look. And when she takes me by the shoulders in her usual greeting, she doesn't smell that way either.

"Are you sick? Maybe this is a bad time for me to come."

"Heavens no, Amanda. People in the city don't get

up with the chickens. Except your grandparents. They've probably had you witness every sunrise since you got here."

"Oh, no. I've slept later here than I've ever slept in my life. I don't have to pump water or fry apples—"

"That's right," Aunt Laura cuts in. "I forget that morning requires breakfast, too. I've heard that the sun coming up looks like a fried egg. Disgusting, but I expect that explains it.

"Actually it's good you've had breakfast, because we're going to be a bit delayed. I thought we could have cold beef for lunch, but Cresswell decided that wasn't good enough for company, so he's gone in search of something better. Put your umbrella down and come have a seat."

I look for an umbrella stand like Omie's or a milk can like we have at home, but I don't find any, so I just lay the dripping thing down.

Aunt Laura leads me into the straw-chair room. Sure enough, she's changed it. The chair is by the window, and, in its place, there's a yellow loveseat with a trunk in front for a table. I sit on the loveseat, but wish I had the straw chair. Aunt Laura leans back in it like a tired queen.

"Has Uncle Cress gone to a restaurant or the grocery?"

"Neither. Or, in a sense, both. He went to a delicatessen."

She waits to see if I know what that is.

"It's a place which sells cooked food to take home. Cress says with this rain we need something hot. But there's no telling what it'll be. Except expensive. Cress's tastes run high."

She stops a minute, picks at lint on her robe.

"So Amanda, your visit to the big city is almost over. Are you ready to go back to Beanburg?"

"It's Goose Rock. And it's not the end of the world, you know." I'm amazed to hear those words come out of my mouth. "We have books and school and—a rosewood piano."

Here I am boasting about the piano when every time we move I wonder why we keep it. Long before moving day the piano is loaded into its wooden crate to be ready when the best chance comes. There has to be full daylight, no rain, and still Daddy worries the whole way that it's going to fall out of the wagon. Once we're settled it has to be unpacked and tuned. Then the crate turns back into a playhouse and the piano collects new dust.

Aunt Laura smiles. "I know Rena kept her piano, 'if only as a hostage against hard times.' That's what she told Mother. I say times are already hard if she doesn't get to play."

"She plays Christmas carols. And in the summer, Mrs. Holcomb brings her chautauqua to Manchester. It's a little festival, with readings and music and poetry, two or three nights in a row."

"No doubt that's just what Manchester needs. And we need some refreshment. Let me fix something to hold us till Cress gets here."

I guess it's a dressing gown she's got on. People here probably wear those all day.

In a minute she comes back carrying two big glasses of orange juice.

"The one with the cherry is yours. I looked for some crackers, too, but there don't seem to be any."

Her hand shakes as she holds out my glass.

"To your health and your travels, Amanda," she says, lifting her drink. "May they both take you far."

I touch my glass to hers.

We sit for a few minutes sipping our juice, and then the front door opens and it's Uncle Cress behind two big sacks. He carries them through the parlor to the kitchen without even saying hello. Uncle Cress is tall and usually walks with a swagger, but today he's round-shouldered. And his blond hair, always neat and shiny, looks like straw.

"All right," he calls from the kitchen, "we'll be ready to eat in a minute. Somebody in this house knows how to treat a guest."

Cold silence. Then he goes on.

"You're pretty special, Mandy, when I have to drag your Aunt Laura out of the bed to see you."

"That's okay."

"And find she's asked you to a lunch of old roast with the fat stiffened on it."

"I don't mind, Uncle Cress, really." I hope he will stop.

"And not a drop to drink in this house. Nothing. And do you know why?"

"Cress—" Aunt Laura begins.

"Because your lovely Aunt Laura is a sot. Yes, she is. Went to bed drinking from a jar and woke up pickled."

Uncle Cress laughs hard but it doesn't cover the clink of ice.

"Don't pay him any mind, Amanda. I'm afraid your Uncle Cress is a bit spoiled."

She almost whispers this last, but Uncle Cress booms right back, "Spoiled! That's a fine thing for you to say, Laura Culton. Who expects her toenails clipped onto a silver platter?"

Aunt Laura giggles. "Isn't he wild?"

She drinks her juice straight down.

After more rustling, Uncle Cress hollers, "Come and get it!" and we walk into the other room. He's brought in folding chairs and heaped the card table with paper cartons. I look for a plate.

"Our guest will have to help herself to a saucer or a soup plate, since the charming Miss L. can't wash a dish."

"I thought you had a maid." I didn't mean to say that.

"This is her week off," Aunt Laura says, searching through a box of barbequed chicken.

Uncle Cress snorts. "Her year off, don't you mean? Even the fullest glass gets empty sometime, Mandy. I can't support Miss Laura and her servant habits forever."

Aunt Laura spoons ice into her juice glass and fills it with something clear.

"Some men go to work, Cresswell. Most men don't expect to quench the lifelong thirst of two people from one glass."

All he says is, "It lasts a lot longer if you don't have one person guzzling."

I try to eat, but my stomach hurts and everything tastes like sand. There's nothing to drink but what's in the bottles, clear for Aunt Laura and amber for Uncle Cress. I take some ice and wait for it to melt.

Uncle Cress eats like a starved horse but Aunt Laura just picks at her chicken wing and crumbles her roll. Only her drink is disappearing.

All of a sudden tears roll down her cheeks—no sound, just two streams of water. Then, without finishing the tears, she starts to laugh. It's a horrible sound, high and broken. I want to do something to stop it, to help her, but I'm frozen. In one motion Uncle Cress stands up, leans across the table, and slaps her hard on the cheek. The flat crack of his hand on her face cuts off the laughter. I jerk back as if he hit me too. Then he walks around the table, picks Aunt Laura up, and carries her out. She can't weigh much, but Uncle Cress is still off balance. His footsteps falter all the way back to their room.

The rain is pouring now and Omie's bright house seems as far away as the moon. I'm scared to move. What if they hear me and come back? What if they don't? But I can't just sit here. I'll put away the food and clean up the kitchen. That might be a little help. If they're not back when I finish, I'll leave a note and take the streetcar home.

I've never been in Aunt Laura's kitchen, but I don't hesitate. Dishes can pile up pretty high with six children, and I've helped out at the Skidmores', too. Here there's just Aunt Laura and Uncle Cress. I push through the swinging door.

There's not a countertop to be seen—it's all dishes. Not cleared and stacked; piled any which way, with food still on them. Before I get close enough to see, I hear the scurry of roaches. I want to turn and run.

Instead, I find the sink and lift its load of dishes to the floor. I draw water to heat on the stove.

Then I see the empty wood box and panic. In this rain I'll never find dry wood. Could they have a water heater like Omie's? I turn on the spigot to see. Sure enough, the water begins steaming. Hot water gives me hope.

I look at each plate hard, like it could keep me from thinking of Aunt Laura. I scour the glasses. There's no room in here for clean dishes, so I find a tablecloth and spread it on the dining room floor. When I finish there's enough stuff for a congregational dinner. I scrub the counters and wash the floor. Three times. It doesn't make me feel any better.

Shelf paper is all I can find for a note. But what can I say?

Aunt Laura,
Gone home. Hope you feel better. Do not worry.

Mandy

I don't put *Love* and I don't put *Amanda.* I can't.

24

 At the streetcar stop I have to wait in the rain. What am I going to say to Omie? She'll want to hear about the visit and it's not for me to tell.

But when I get there Opie's describing a mill accident. By the time he gets through, supper is ready. Maybe I'll get by—

"And how did you find Miss Laura?" he asks, first thing.

"Easy. She's right where you said she'd be."

"And did she feed you ambrosia?"

I think it's Aunt Laura he's poking fun at, but I'm not sure.

"Chicken."

"The bird of the gods."

"Samuel—"

Opie lowers his head.

"Uncle Cress brought in food," I offer.

"Money's a good cook." He goes back to his soup.

We eat in silence except for silverware clinking and

the creak of Opie's chair. Then Omie gets up to pour coffee.

"We're going to miss you, Mandy," she says, coming around behind me. "I can't believe the time has gone so fast."

"I'll miss you, too. And Memphis and this house—" I look at the dining room, its pale blue walls and high rail holding Omie's plate collection. There are flowers, fruit, birds—even a naked lady with cherubs dancing around her.

"But I promised your mother I wouldn't keep you. And you must be getting homesick."

She kisses the top of my head, then goes around to Opie.

"Who would have thought we'd be borrowing children?" he asks, as she fills his cup.

"They're every one borrowed," she tells him.

I can't help but think of the last table I sat at. The crowd of boxes, Aunt Laura's wild laugh. I wonder how she imagined her life those years when she ate at this table. And Mama, too. What was she dreaming? Sawmill gravy and a rented house full of kids?

"Amanda," Omie's voice is gentle. "You must be wool-gathering."

She's holding out a sauce dish, something to put on pound cake.

Embarrassed I ask, "When you make pound cake do you cream the sugar and butter with your hand?"

That's what Mama does. Takes a big bowl in the bedroom, rocks the cradle with her foot. Even with Willie.

"Of course she does," Opie answers. "And sings 'Love Lifted Me' for as long as it takes."

"I do not. Sometimes I sing 'Softly and Tenderly.' "

"Only hymns that have to do with cakes."

They tease each other like Mama and Daddy. I didn't know that was a blessing.

After dinner Omie comes up to help me pack. "I owe you an apology, Mandy," she says. "Whatever happened today was partly my fault."

I feel like someone took a stitch in the middle of me.

"What do you mean?"

"I expect there was a scene at Laura's—"

"Oh, no. Everything was—"

"You can't protect me, honey. I've seen my share."

"It's not your fault."

"Be that as it may, you didn't have to see it. I'm afraid I put you in harm's way, used you like your mother did the ring."

"What ring?"

"And I should have known better. It's just that I don't see any way to help her. She won't come near me. And I thought maybe you, being Rena's daughter—maybe she'd reach out to you and that would help her find herself. I know it's foolish—" Omie sits on the bed, puts her head in her hands. Her voice catches. "I don't know what will become of her."

Does this mean Mama didn't suggest my coming—it was all Omie's idea? Not for me but for Aunt Laura?

"She's been awfully good to me," I say.

"She *is* good," Omie insists. "Why, when Laura was a child, she had the clearest, deepest eyes you ever saw. And she'd look for hours at a picture or a flower or straight into your face. Whatever she had, she'd give you; whatever she knew, she'd tell you. She sang if she was happy, she wailed if she was hurt, she laughed like laughing was all she had to do in this world."

"She still has that laugh."

"Yes, but it has another sound entirely. Oh, you can't expect a child to stay a child, 'trailing clouds of glory.' But Laura's not just grown, she's changed completely. And I held you out to her, hoping she'd turn around—"

"What about the ring?"

"It worked for your mother. But gold and emerald aren't the same as flesh and blood."

Omie stops right where she should go on.

"But what happened?" I think back to that summer night, Mama big with Willie, me angry about second-hand clothes. "I know Mama ordered a ring but she told me it was for her, that she needed something pretty."

"No doubt, but the little emerald was for your father, for the mill. She told Ostriker's she wanted it on approval, then used it to secure a loan Jim had applied for. He didn't know why the bank finally came through, but it meant he could buy trees."

"Didn't she have to pay for the ring?"

"I think she made one or two payments—you know your mother, she didn't tell me about it at the time—

but then she sent the ring back. She'd gotten enough money to prime the pump, so to speak, and business was flowing. Of course your Daddy didn't know."

I remember how she made me promise not to tell him. And I thought she was selfish! Tears sting my eyes.

"I'm so sorry, Mandy."

"It's not that—"

"I should have known better. You remind me of her, too."

"Mama?"

"No, Laura."

"That's what she said."

I see Aunt Laura at her dressing table, perfect as a flower. "I used to look just like you," she said. And we talked, with her clothes heaped around us and Beale Street ahead. Was that just the day before yesterday?

"I didn't believe her," I tell Omie.

"You wouldn't."

She pushes the suitcase aside and hugs me.

"I don't want you to think I asked you to visit just for Laura's sake. I wanted to see you."

"I know."

But it does seem like I came for a crowd of people: Omie and Laura, Mama and Willie and me. I'm glad I did, though. Mr. Aden says travel always teaches. That's not the half of it.

25

It's the path I always take when I've been up to my thinking rock. It follows the wet-weather spring down behind the house. In the dream it's slippery as April and I grab at saplings to keep my balance.

For some cause I'm in a big rush and when I run up on the porch and find the front door locked, I don't even stop to wonder, just tear around to the back. They can't have all gone off. Maybe there's a bedroom window open.

I squeeze between the snowball bush and the house but it's no use. The window is shut tight. And I can see the house isn't empty. There's a heap of quilts on the bed and Mama under them. There's the cradle within arm's reach. And between the bed and the window, all across the bare floor, is a dark pool.

"Mama!"

I scramble from behind the branches right into a little rose bush. Get free from that, scoop up a rock, and climb the porch rail. There's no latch. I have to break the window in the door. I have to make it big enough to get through.

Glass scrapes my wrists.

"Mama! Mama!"

I smash the glass again and again.

Hands are on my face, smoothing back my hair.

"There, Mandy."

Someone's sitting me up, holding me close. I push at the arms.

"I have to get through. There's blood."

"It's all right—"

"No, it's Mama. There's blood—"

"It's only a dream, Amanda."

Omie's voice gathers me back. "I'm right here. It was just a dream."

"But it wasn't a dream! It really happened—"

"I know it seems that way—"

"It *did* happen, only not to me. It was Mrs. Skidmore who found her and broke the window—"

"Mandy, what are you talking about?"

I'm wide awake now.

"Mama, when Willie was born. Daddy and Doc Bailey left, and if Mrs. Skidmore hadn't come and seen the blood—"

"Slow down. What blood?"

"All over the bedroom floor. She saw it through the window, thought it was water leaking from the icebox, but I knew in the dream and I broke the doorglass, just like she did, but I couldn't get through."

I feel frantic again. There's a big hurt in my throat; it's hard to breathe.

"There, there, honey. It's all over now."

"But if Mrs. Skidmore hadn't found Mama and sent her husband for help, Mama would have died, locked up in that house. And maybe Willie, too. And all I thought about was having to quit school—"

"What?"

"How it was unfair, me having to stay home and take care of them."

"I didn't know that."

"I didn't tell anybody."

"I mean I didn't know you stayed home."

"You didn't? I thought that's why Mama asked if I could visit. I've not had a day of school since Willie came."

"Well, this is the first I've heard about that *or* the hemorrhage. Jim just wrote that Rena was weak, needed all of you to help with chores." Omie's voice thickens. "That child would die of thirst before she'd ask for a drink of water."

"What do you mean?"

"I would have come, child. I could have taken care of her and that baby, too. Lord knows, I've bottomed enough babies. But Rena wouldn't ask, or Jim Perritt. Proud as poplars, the two of them."

She draws herself up, pulls her flowered robe around her.

"So you've looked after a baby and nursed an invalid and run a household, and Opie and I have been treating you like a child. We must have tried your patience, Mandy."

"No, it's fun to be a child again."

We both laugh.

"Would you like some hot milk? I don't think I can lie right down after such a tale as this."

I follow Omie into the night-lit hall and down the staircase. It's much longer in the dark. On the landing the full moon peers through the window like a face.

"The first thing I remember about you," I whisper to Omie, "is when you held me up to that window. 'It's an oculus window,' you told me, 'like your eye.' I thought you meant that's where the house looked out."

Omie smiles as she turns on the kitchen light. We both blink.

"That sounds like one of Laura's notions."

"Or Helen's."

"It just goes to show we're all related."

"I guess so."

I think about that while she heats the milk. Mama and Omie, Aunt Laura and Helen and me. Like a crazy quilt stitched and bound together, not the same pattern, not even the same cloth. Old tie silk, velvet, scraps of wool—

"Here you go."

Omie sets two night-blue mugs on the table.

"I added a little honey."

"It smells good."

The bubbles make me think of fresh milk, how it froths at the rim of the pail. And how this time tomorrow night I'll be home.

26

 The train leaves at seven-thirty, so we're up before light. My talk with Omie seems like a dream. With the other dream inside it.

"Morning, Miss Perritt," Opie says when I come into the kitchen.

"Is it?" I ask, bleary-eyed.

"Your grandmother says you had to sit up half the night and talk. Womenfolks! Here, let me get you some coffee."

He pours me a cup, takes a look at the toast in the stove.

" 'Don't let it burn,' your grandmother says, as if I had a handle on fire."

"I'll watch it."

The pieces come out, golden and yellow.

"I'm going home today, Opie."

"Really? I thought we were putting a package on that train."

"I'm going to see Mama and Willie—"

"Fetch some of Omie's preserves, please ma'am."

"And Daddy and Helen—"

"They're in the pantry. Blackberry. In the jam jar."

"I'm really going to see them, Opie."

"You'd better eat up then. You won't see them if we're still here when it's light."

"That's what I know," Omie says, as she comes in wearing her robe. "I'm awfully slow this morning. If you don't mind, Mandy, I'll let Opie take you to the station. I'm getting too old to say good-bye."

"Too old for talking till the sky pales," he teases.

"You won't mind?"

"No, Omie. I'm sorry I kept you up."

"That's all right, child. You can't plan dreams." She sets out plates. We eat quickly and Opie gets my coat.

"Button that up," he says. "It's cold as Christmas this morning."

"You write me now, Mandy," Omie orders. "And tell Rena to let me know how she is. Tell her what I told you." She straightens my collar. "And tell Jim not to make himself such a stranger. Surely he can come out of the woods long enough to say hello."

"We've got to go, Anna."

"And kiss that baby for me, and hug everybody who'll stand still—"

"Anna—"

"And here's some ribbon candy. For the trip."

"Thank you, Omie. Thank you for everything."

She hugs me close. Opie's already headed for the car.

* * *

He leans forward to hurry us through the traffic. "Never saw a woman who could leave." He wipes our breath off the windshield.

"Aunt Laura can. She just disappears."

No comment.

"Opie, would you tell her good-bye for me?"

"If she ever darkens my door."

It wouldn't have to be darkening, I want to say, remembering curtains and beads in the doorways of her house.

We're coming up on Union Station now. Opie cranes his neck, hunting a place to park.

"And Opie—"

"What, Traveler?"

"Try to get to the ocean."

For a minute he looks confused, then it comes back. "I'll try. But first I've got to get you on this train."

While Opie checks the schedule board in the lobby, I listen: heels tap marble, clothes rustle, conversations swoop by like birds. Then, a voice from the wall: "*Passenger service now boarding on track nine for Chattanooga, Knoxville, and points north. All aboard, please.*"

From behind a big woman in a yellow coat, Opie appears.

"That's your train, Mandy. We're just under the wire."

He takes my hand and we snake through the crowd and down the steps to the concourse. Opie hails a porter.

"Have a safe trip and don't stay away so long."

"I'll try not to. Thank you for having me."

People push between us. I can't tell if he says something else or if he's just nodding.

"Good-bye, Opie!" No one can hear me. "Good-bye, Memphis. Good-bye!"

27

Good-bye is always hello to something else. Good-bye/hello, good-bye/hello, like the sound of a rocking chair. The train pulls out and Memphis slips away: Omie, Opie, Aunt Laura, the man who played the bird horn.

Across the aisle an old woman is saying the rosary. I know what it is because Janey Mobeltini brought hers to school. Mr. Aden asked her to explain it.

"Each bead is a prayer," she told us. "We say one Our Father and ten Hail Marys—"

"But to whom are you praying?"

"The Queen of Heaven."

"Why not to God?"

"He's busy."

Mr. Aden said you're supposed to know the prayers so well that they keep the top of your mind busy, and free the rest to "contemplate the Mysteries: Joyful, Sorrowful, and Glorious." Janey said she didn't know about that.

I wonder what Mysteries the old woman is thinking of, with her red headscarf on and her hanky balled up in her hand. I've got a load of Mysteries. I look at my ticket and remember how I explained round trip to Helen. "You come back the same way you went." I was so grown-up. I knew all about it.

"But that's not round, that's straight," Helen said.

"It's just a way of talking," I told her.

It's not. It's a Mystery. You don't ever come back the same. The tracks are spiked down and the train stays on the track, but you come back from a different direction entirely. It makes me sleepy just to think about it.

When I wake up the news butch is coming through. "Papers, candy, souvenirs," he calls. "Sandwiches, soda pop!"

Now is my chance to get presents. I wait while the man in front buys cigarettes.

Would the boys like the glass engines I saw on the trip down? What about all-day suckers for the girls? I should have thought about this before. Now it's my turn.

"Something for you, Missy?"

"Yes, but I'm not sure . . . Is that a whistle?"

"Yes ma'am. Penny whistle. Knows every tune ever played." He picks one up, puts it to his mustached mouth, and makes it shriek. The rosary lady stirs. "Penny whistle, cost you a nickel," he tells me.

Whistles are better than suckers. They last. "And the engines?"

"A quarter, except for this granddaddy." He lifts a big one out of the pile. "Fifty cents for this."

"I'll take two engines, two whistles, and—do you have anything for a baby?"

He reaches into his shirt pocket. "Balloons, penny apiece."

"I'll take three. Are those news magazines?" They're rolled up, stuck in the back of his tray.

"*Time.* That's fifteen cents."

"All right." That will do for Daddy. "One more thing. What do you have for a lady?"

"Sand," he says, fishing in the tray for a tiny bottle. "Seven layers, four colors." He holds it up.

"We've got rocks prettier than that." That's rude but true. "I'm sorry. Do you have anything else?"

"Red flower." He finds another bottle with a little rose inside. "Fifty cents." Mama might like that on the kitchen windowsill.

"I'll take that too. That's all."

He slips a paper bag from under the tray and fills it. "One dollar even with tax."

We trade. The seat next to me is empty so I lay out my purchases. I can't wait to see Helen with the whistle. And Willie's eyes when I blow up the balloons. I'm really going home!

I pack the presents up and set out for the dining car. I like to see if I can balance without touching the seats. Going between cars, I hold my breath and look down at the speeding ground.

All they're serving now is coffee and pie. That's all right. I really just want to sit here. It's the most magical part of the train, the dining car. To be sitting at a table, eating, and all the world flying past.

Somebody loves this land we're rushing through, every little hill, each house, each tree. Looks for it the way I look for Goose Rock. It doesn't mean I'll stay there forever.

I want to ask Mama about her music. Maybe we could work out time for her to play. I get time to do my school work. So do the boys. And we know how to do housekeeping.

Mama may say her need for music is all in Aunt Laura's head. There's no telling. She might decide to give lessons or sell the piano and turn all that song into trees. On the way to Memphis I would have said I knew Mama. But she's as much a mystery as Aunt Laura. Maybe everyone is.

It's getting dark as we come into the mountains, just enough light left to tell when we go through the Gap. The moon is like a big mother-of-pearl button.

> *I see the moon and the moon sees me.*
> *The moon sees the somebody I want to see. . . .*

I used to think I couldn't belong to a family so far back in the sticks. "We'd call it the jumping off place," Daddy says, "but the hills are too close together to jump." Now I see a family isn't one thing or one place. Tonight I'm glad to know home is waiting. Home and the world, too.

I guess I fell asleep again. It must be midnight. I can't make out much but I think we're almost there. The shape of the hills feels right. And surely that's Hensley's farm. Yes, because the train brakes just came on. That huddle of buildings is Manchester.

I gather my belongings and take a deep breath. Who will be there? Just Daddy? I can see the depot lights.

For a minute I close my eyes. I don't want to lose Memphis. Then the brakes hiss again. My heart jumps and my eyes fly open.

There they stand, the whole lot of them! David and Ben almost as tall as Daddy, Mama small and solid. Look at Willie, holding his head away from her shoulder, trying to turn around. He's wearing a bonnet. Everyone is waving. Helen tugs at Anna and jumps up and down.

When the train stops, Mama hands Willie to Daddy. I can see her at the steps as I walk the length of the car. She's made this trip so many times. I wonder if it's been hard for her to come back.

"Welcome home, city girl," she says, holding out her arms.

"Hello, Mama."